D0058195

The Man Who Gave
Thunder to the Earth

The Man Who Gave Thunder to the Earth

A TAOS WAY OF SEEING AND UNDERSTANDING

By Nancy Wood

DOUBLEDAY & COMPANY, INC., GARDEN CITY, NEW YORK

1976

The introductory piece, "The Vast Old Religion of Taos," was extracted from an article entitled "New Mexico," by D. H. Lawrence, which appeared in the book *Phoenix*, published by William Heinemann, Ltd., London, and in the United States in *Phoenix I: The Posthumous Papers of D. H. Lawrence*, edited by Edward McDonald. Copyright © 1936 by Frieda Lawrence, copyright © renewed 1964 by the estate of the late Frieda Lawrence Ravagli. All rights reserved. Reprinted by permission of The Viking Press, Laurence Pollinger Ltd., and the estate of the late Mrs. Frieda Lawrence.

Library of Congress Cataloging in Publication Data
Wood, Nancy C
  The man who gave thunder to the earth.
  I. Title.
PZ4.W877Man   [PS3573.O595]   813'.5'4
ISBN 0-385-09682-8
Library of Congress Catalog Card Number 75–30462

CONTENTS

Expansion

Full Circle

THE VAST OLD RELIGION OF TAOS

From an article by D. H. Lawrence

I think New Mexico was the greatest experience from the outside world that I have ever had. It certainly changed me forever. Curious as it may sound, it was New Mexico that liberated me from the present era of civilization, the great era of material and mechanical development. Months spent in Holy Kandy, in Ceylon, the holy of holies of southern Buddhism had not touched the great psyche of materialism and idealism which dominated me. And years, even in the exquisite beauty of Sicily, right among the old Greek paganism that still lives there, had not shattered the essential Christianity on which my character was estalished. . . .

The moment I saw the brilliant proud morning shine high up over the deserts of Santa Fe, something stood still in my soul, and I started to attend. There was a certain magnificence in the high-up day, a certain eagle-like royalty, so different from the equally pure, equally pristine and lovely morning of Australia, which is so soft, so utterly pure in its softness, and betrayed by green parrots flying. But in the lovely morning of Australia one went into a dream. In the magnificent fierce morning of New Mexico one sprang awake, a new part of the soul woke up suddenly, and the old world gave way to a new. . . .

For a greatness of beauty I have never experienced anything like New Mexico. All those mornings when I went with a hoe along the ditch to the canyon, at the ranch, and stood, in the fierce, proud silence of the Rockies, or their foot-hills, to look far over the desert to the blue mountains away in Arizona, blue as chalcedony, with the sagebrush desert sweeping gray-blue in between, dotted with tiny cube-crystals of houses: the vast amphitheater of lofty, indomitable desert, sweeping round to the ponderous Sangre de Cristo Mountains on the east, and coming up flush at the pine-dotted foot-hills of the Rockies! What splendor! Only the tawny eagle could really sail out into the splendor of it all. Leo Stein once wrote to me: "It is the most aesthetically satisfying landscape I know."—To me it was much more than that.

It had a splendid, silent terror, and a vast, far-and-wide magnificence which made it way beyond mere aesthetic appreciation. Never is the light more pure and overweening than there, arching with a royalty almost cruel over the hollow, uptilted world. For it is curious that the land which has produced modern political democracy at its highest pitch should give one the greatest sense of overwhelming, terrible proudness and mercilessness: but so beautiful. God! so beautiful! Those that have spent morning after morning alone there pitched among the pines above the great proud world of desert will know, almost unbearably, how beautiful it is, how clear and unquestioned is the might of the day. Just day itself is tremendous there. It is so easy to understand that the Aztecs gave hearts of men to the sun. For the sun is not merely hot or scorching, not at all. It is of a brilliant and unchallengeable purity and haughty serenity which would make one sacrifice the heart to it. Ah, yes, in New Mexico the heart is sacrificed to the sun, and the human being is left stark, heartless, but undauntedly religious. . . .

For religion is an experience, an uncontrollable, sensual experience even more so than love: I use sensual to mean an experience deep down in the senses, inexplicable and inscrutable. . . .

I had no permanent feeling of religion till I came to New Mexico and penetrated into the old human race-experience there. It is curious that it should be in America, of all places, that a European should really experience religion, after touching the old Mediterranean and the East. It is curious that one should get a sense of living religion from the Red Indians, having failed to get it from Hindus or Sicilian Catholics or Chinghalese. . . .

For the Red Indian seems to me much older than Greeks or Hindus or any European or even Egyptians. The Red Indian, as a civilized and truly religious man, civilized beyond tabu and totem, as he is in the south, is religious in perhaps the oldest sense, and deepest, of the world. That is to say, he is a remnant of the most deeply religious race still living. So it seems to me. . . .

But while a tribe retains its religion and keeps up its religious practices, and while any member of the tribe shares in those practices, then there is a tribal integrity and a living tradition going back far beyond the birth of Christ, beyond the pyramids, beyond Moses. A vast, old religion which once swayed the earth lingers in unbroken practice there in New Mexico older, perhaps, than anything in the world save Australian aboriginal tabu and totem, and that is not yet religion.

You can feel it, the atmosphere of it, around the pueblos.

Not, of course, when the place is crowded with sightseers and motor cars. But go to Taos pueblo on some brilliant snowy morning, and see the white figures on the roof, or come riding through at dusk on some windy evening, when the black skirts of the silent women blow around the white wide boots, and you will feel the old, old root of human consciousness still reaching down to depths we know nothing of; and of which, only too often, we are jealous. It seems it will not be long before the pueblos are uprooted.

But never shall I forget watching the dancers, the men with the fox-skin swaying down from their buttocks, file out at San Geronimo, and the women with seed-rattles following. The long, streaming glistening black hair of the men. Even in ancient Crete long hair was sacred in a man, as it is still in the Indians. Never shall I forget the utter absorption of the dance, so quiet, so steadily, timelessly rhythmic, and silent, with the ceaseless down-tread, always to the earth's center, the very reverse of the upflow of Dionysiac or Christian ecstasy. Never shall I forget the deep singing of the men at the drum, swelling and sinking, the deepest sound I have heard in all my life, deeper than thunder, deeper than the sound of the Pacific Ocean, deeper than the roar of a deep waterfall: the wonderful deep sound of men calling to the unspeakable depths. . . .

Never shall I forget the Christmas dances at Taos, twilight, snow, the darkness coming over the great wintry mountains and the lonely pueblo, then suddenly, again, like dark calling dark, the deep Indian cluster-singing around the drum, wild and awful, suddenly rousing on the lost dusk as the procession starts. And then the bonfires leaping suddenly in pure spurts of high flame, columns of sudden flame forming an alley for the procession. . . .

Never shall I forget the Indian races, when the young men, even the boys run naked, smeared with white earth and stuck with bits of eagle fluff for the swiftness of the heavens, and the old men brush them with eagle feathers, to give them power. And they run in the strange hurling fashion of the primitive world, hurled forward, not making speed deliberately. And the race is not for victory. It is not a contest. There is no competition. It is a great cumulative effort. The tribe this day is adding up its male energy and exerting to the utmost: for what? To get power, to get strength: to come, by sheer cumulative hurling effort of the bodies of men, into contact with the great cosmic source of vitality which gives strength, power, energy to the men who can grasp it, energy for the year of attainment.

It was a vast old religion, greater than anything we know: more darkly and nakedly religious. There is no God, no conception of a god. All is god. But it is not the pantheism we are accustomed to, which expresses itself as "God is everywhere, God is in everything."

In the oldest religion, everything was alive, not supernaturally but naturally alive. There were only deeper and deeper streams of life, vibrations of life more and more vast. So rocks were alive, but a mountain had a deeper, vaster life than a rock, and it was much harder for a man to bring his spirit, or his energy into contact with the life of the mountain, as from a great standing well of life, than it was to come into contact with the rock. And he had to put forth a greater religious effort.

For the whole life-effort of man was to get his life into direct contact with the elemental life of the cosmos, mountain-life, cloud-life, thunder-life, air-life, earth-life, sun-life. To come into immediate felt contact, and so derive energy, power and a dark sort of joy. This effort into sheer naked contact, without an intermediary or mediator, is the real meaning of religion. And at the sacred races the runners hurled themselves in a terrible cumulative effort, through the air, to come at last into naked contact with the very life of the air, which is the life of the clouds, and so of the rain.

It was a vast and pure religion, without idols or images, even mental ones. It is the oldest religion, a cosmic religion the same for all people, not broken up into specific gods or saviors or systems. It is the religion which precedes the god-concept and is therefore greater and deeper than any god-religion.

And it lingers still, for a little while in New Mexico but long enough to have been a revelation to me. And the Indian, however objectionable he may be on occasion, has still some of the strange beauty and pathos of the religion that brought him forth and is now shedding him away into oblivion. . . .

But there it is: the newest democracy ousting the oldest religion! And once the oldest religion is ousted, one feels the democracy and all its paraphernalia will collapse, and the oldest religion, which comes down to us from man's pre-war days, will start again. The skyscraper will scatter on the winds like thistledown, and the genuine America, the America of New Mexico will start on its course again. This is an interregnum.

D. H. LAWRENCE
1931

Identification

THE PEOPLE
OF THE SUN HOUSE MOON

He was an Old Man without a name or if he had a name it was not repeated or remembered, even by himself.

The place where the Old Man lived was just a village in the sun which had been there for so long that it took on the color and appearance of the earth. It smelled like the earth for it was made of the earth and went back into the earth when its time was through. The village was a way for the people to live surrounded by the earth on six sides. The color and dryness of the people was the same as their village made of earth and generation.

The village was old and the people were old. The people looked like the First People and the Last People. They were called the People of the Sun House Moon. They planted and reaped and planted again, on and on, from one time to another time, in the same way always so that nothing ever changed. The People of the Sun House Moon were not a people of change even though the world they lived in changed. They were a People of One Way which was unchangeable.

The Old Man lived among them for their whole time upon the earth and remained long after. He was there waiting when the People of the Sun House Moon came out of the earth and stood at the base of the Mountain. He told them to live there among the trees, beside a stream flowing down from the mountaintop where there was something good to see no matter what direction they looked. It was a place of tall grass and rich soil. It was where the sun and rain took turns in coming down. It was where the earth and sky formed a Seam for the people to live upon. The Seam was a place of strength for it had both earth and sky within it.

The Old Man taught the People of the Sun House Moon how to plant, for the Spirit of the Corn was in him and he was able to make things grow. He gave them the gift of Fire and stood guard over it so that it never went out nor was stolen nor spread farther than the village itself. The Old Man and the Fire were always side by side. Even in the dark everyone could tell where the Old Man was.

But the Old Man wanted to do more than guard the Fire and make the corn grow. There was a story inside him that he wanted to leave behind for the sake of what he had found out. He wanted to carve his story in stone or write it in the sky or tell it to the water and it would be only him and the stones and the sky and the water and the story he had inside him that needed saying.

The Old Man wanted to capture the wind and keep its song for the rest of the world to hear and it would be for him to decide when the music needed playing.

The Old Man wanted to give Thunder to the earth and teach it to speak in a new voice in a language that was yet to come.

The Old Man wanted to punctuate the world with silence.

He waited to be heard, not having the means to be heard nor a way to capture the wind nor a plan to take thunder from the sky. He had his thoughts for company but words were always after them and so his thoughts fell out of place and his words became imitations of his ideas.

The Old Man walked in opposite worlds, hearing an opposite tune. He felt himself divided even though he was at home in one of these worlds and in the other he was not. He already knew which world was important and which was not. The Old Man perceived that both worlds were always present and that it was only a matter of choice.

The Old Man called them the First and Second Worlds of Being.

The Old Man could leave the First World any time he wanted to because it was the practical world; it was the world of everyday things. The Old Man could go into the Second World and stay there because it was the world of dreams and hope; it was the world of regeneration. The Old Man perceived that without this world he would perish; he perceived that without the First World he would merely die.

The Old Man traveled back and forth between these two worlds, using the First World when he needed to eat and the Second World when he needed sustenance. The Old Man used the First World for sleep and the Second World for rest. He used the First World for a ticket to his destination but the Second World was the means he traveled by.

Now when the New People came into the Old Man's world, he was still young and riding on the backs of stars to see what the other side of the moon looked like. He was gathering up rainbows to keep the colors for his eyes and taking the softness out of rain. In those days, the Old Man wore sunlight braided in his hair and he blew the dust off the moon and wore it on his feet. He took fire from the sun and threw it across the sky in order to see beyond; he tipped the clouds to one side in order to see around.

When he came home, the Old Man began to see things as they were right there. He began to see what the New People had done in his absence.

The New People came from the east, the Direction of Understanding, but brought no Understanding with them.

They went to the west, the Direction of Growing, but no growth took place in them.

The New People went to the north, the Direction of Introspection, but did not look inside themselves.

They went to the south, the Direction of Comfort and Belonging, but found no comfort there nor did they truly belong.

The New People went out in all directions, devouring everything. They devoured the green forests and the yellow grass. They devoured tall mountains and flowing rivers. They devoured the oceans and continents and looked for ways to devour the sky. The New People devoured the Old People until at last there were only a few of them left. The New People wanted to devour those also. They saw no value to them.

So it was when the New People looked at him, they saw just an Old Man, weathered and bent, with one leg longer than the other so that he limped along. It was an effort for him to go anywhere even though he had no place to go nor was his direction clear. Sometimes he would draw up his legs and try to fly, lifting his whole body toward the sky, making his arms into wings. He would sing like a bird and begin to perceive everything from above so he would not have to see what the New People had done.

Looking at him, the New People saw him falling down each time he tried to fly. They did not see that he had discarded the container that was his body and had left the First World for a time. They did not see that he could become a blackbird if he wanted to.

The Old Man always appeared to be moving even when he was standing still. He was always in motion even when he was lying on the ground. The energy that the Old Man had was the energy of a river flowing on to the sea. It was the energy of wind released and homeless and the energy of a single drop of rain. He had the energy of a star leaving a crowded night and the energy of a leaf turning yellow in the fall. He had the energy of new flowers unfolding their petals and the energy of an embryo being born. He had the energy of an old tree falling down.

The New People sensed the Old Man's energy and did not know what to think of it. The Old Man had the energy to go where he wished and yet he seemed to go nowhere and was exhausted from it. The New People did not understand what he was all about. They only laughed at the sight of him limping and falling or standing still with a puzzled look in his eyes. They laughed because there was no explanation for him.

As the Old Man went along, he always held his head up to the sky as if to drink in the sun through his eyes. The New People noticed that his eyes were dark and strange like storm clouds gathering or a sea that waits for a hurricane. His eyes were never on the ground and he walked through traffic as if it were a field. The New People noticed the way the cars swerved to avoid him and that sometimes the big trucks tried to run him down for being in the way. The Old Man did not seem to care. He went on the way he was, with his face turned toward the sky.

If the Old Man is not careful he will be run over, they said.

But they did not try and save him from the traffic.

The New People dismissed the Old Man from their minds as they dismissed all that was an image from a mirror held too close to time and thus became a continuous reflection of what was meant to be and did not become.

Yet long after they had seen him and gone their way, they would always see him again, sometimes in the middle of the night in a dream without sleep or a sleep too deep for a dream. He always occupied the empty seat on a train or was the isolated passenger on a plane who traveled without baggage or a ticket. He was the stranger on the street whose eyes they could not meet; he was what made them stop in the middle of a deal or made them deal even faster to cover up. The Old Man remained a memory long after he was put out of their minds.

Mostly it was the Old Man's face.

When they looked at him they saw a face they could not explain. It was an old face, older than the oldest man. It had the appearance of being worked on, as rain upon stone or wind upon the uppermost tree on a mountaintop. His face had the worn consideration of stone or wood standing out in the rain. It had the anguish of permanent drought with cracks hollowed out by the earth climbing out of its skin.

But across his face there flickered in a certain light the fresh softness of a boy. They saw something then which was still growing, a face not fully formed or finished. It was a face of expectation and innocence, a face that laughter visited often and was a stranger to doubt. It was a face of openness and trust. It was a face that the First World had not ruined yet and to which the Second World was simply home.

Even that was not all there was to his face.

Under certain conditions of perception, he wore a woman's face which seemed neither young nor old because of the greater depth behind it. It was a face formed by pain and was yet painless; it was a face formed by beauty and was yet not beautiful. It was the face of desire and memory greater than experience. It was a face that love had soothed and nurtured.

The Old Man said:

The face that I am comfortable with is the face you do not see.

It is the face that the fish wore long ago when it swam in a sea which covered the earth.

It is the face that the four-legged animal wore when it came down from a tree and looked around.

It is a face of next year's blossoms and rain that is yet to fall.

It is a face which has only one eye which sees through the dark and into corners being formed by water.

The face that I am comfortable with is the face that is turned inside out. It looks at itself and what you see is a mirror of my inner face. Sometimes, yes, it is sad because I am looking at my own desolation. I am waiting for rain. I am searching for a cloud to reason with but my words are lost in the wind.

There was always this mystery and it too worked its way into his face and formed the deliberation of his eyes. They were eyes that could not be looked into directly for they always asked the question, what are we doing here?

The Old Man's eyes made them focus on the affirmation

of the Second World that they feared and desired equally and on the negation that the First World bequeathed to them as heirs to its futility.

Yet there was another part of the Old Man's appearance which made the New People uneasy. The Old Man always seemed to be carrying a heavy object although there was nothing at all in his hands. He was always bent over from the weight of it or leaning to one side when it went off balance. Sometimes he searched the ground when he dropped it or looked for it in the trees above his head. Sometimes he sat down with his weight, opened his hands, and shouted to the sky.

The New People blamed the Old Man's peculiarities on the fact that within his village everyone married everyone else. The People of the Sun House Moon were not permitted to go outside their village to find a man or a woman to marry. It was a custom they had observed since they came out of the earth in the beginning, carrying the Light of the Great Spirit.

It goes to show, the New People said, what happens when the same blood is passed around. The reason the people of this village behave strangely is because no new bood has ever come in.

For a long time, the New People tried to bring new blood to the Old Man's village. They tried to bring it on wheels to make the People of the Sun House Moon move faster. They tried to bring it on the lips of a new language to make them speaker better. They tried to bring it in boxes of new and unfamiliar objects so the People of the Sun House Moon would want more. The New People tried to make the People of the Sun House Moon feel foolish because of the blood they had which was the blood they wanted to keep.

The New People looked at the Old Man and always saw

in him the greatest example of their failure to mix freshness into the blood of his people. When all the rest of the country was moving along in the direction the New People wanted, the People of the Sun House Moon were moving backward because of their blood which was very old and made from the blood of the earth itself.

Each time the earth was wounded, the People of the Sun House Moon carefully tended to it, gathering the dust from its bleeding cracks and the bones from the places where it opened up. When the earth burned, they gathered ashes when the fire died. When the earth was flooded, they rose on the wings of a giant bird and took one feather from it. All this went into the making of their blood and they were content to keep it as it was.

The New People could not see how much time it had taken to make the blood of the People of the Sun House Moon or what precious things went into it. They could not see that the creation of such blood had forged a certain bond between the People of the Sun House Moon and the world about them. They could not see that the Old Man carried the bond with him, struggling and bending under the weight of it every single day. The Old Man tried to explain the bond as best he could.

The Old Man called it the Thread.

THE THREAD

One day in the fall of the year, the Old Man was standing at the gate to his village as the New People were coming in for the fiesta. Listen to my story, he said. It is a story of worth.

It costs too much to get in, the New People grumbled. What is there to see? They looked around at the poorness of the village and mistook it for poverty.

Every day there is something good to see, the Old Man said, opening his arms. Sometimes the fields are so green they cover the mind with wetness.

The New People noticed the dust and mistook it for filth.

How dirty it is, the New People said, counting out their money, making sure they were given the correct change. How strange the houses are. And look, the children have no shoes. We must buy the children some shoes. They held out money to the Old Man. Buy the children some shoes, they said, mistaking their guilt for generosity.

But the Old Man was looking toward the fields where he had harvested the last of his corn. Sometimes the corn is big enough to crawl inside to see the way it is growing, the Old Man said. Sometimes the water runs backward, taking us to the place where we were born. Sometimes the rainbow breaks in two and a butterfly comes out of the middle.

We want to take pictures, the New People said. How much to take a picture? We'll send you a picture of yourself in color.

The New People began to pick out certain of the Old Man's people, mistaking their beauty for quaintness.

The Thread costs nothing at all, the Old Man said, making them write their names in a book. You have a Thread and I have a Thread. Look and see what my Thread contains.

The New People had their cameras pointed at the rooftops where the People of the Sun House Moon had come out to sit down. They were dressed in splendid clothes of many colors, for the fiesta was the most important event of the year. It was in honor of the patron saint the New People had given to them three hundred years before. Even so, nothing at all had changed. The fiesta for the patron saint fell on the same day that the People of the Sun House Moon always gave thanks to the Yellow Corn Mother for the crop they had just harvested. It had been a good crop and would last all year.

The Old Man drew his red blanket around him, noticing that the New People had turned to him, pressing their cameras to their eyes. He decided to speak to them some more.

That which you are I cannot be. I am myself unique, even though I am made of the same material as you. Different things have gone into the making of my Thread. All things were available to me and I went along choosing them. Everything is part of the Thread.

A little more to the left, the New People said.

Some things were the right things and some were not, the Old Man said. But everything went into the making of my Thread, even what I brought with me at my birth. I brought what I had learned from all the other lives I had lived. I could not remember any of the experiences of those lives. What came with me was Essence which is a way of seeing and understanding. It is intuition and imagination of the wildest sort. Everything is part of the Thread.

Where is the bathroom? the New People asked. Where is a place to eat?

The Old Man reached up and pulled down the Thread for them to see. Here, he said. Look at the amazing things in the Thread. Every movement of nature is there, living and dying without effort.

The One-Eyed Bird who speaks with Thunder, the One-Eyed Bird is there.

The Four-Legged Buffalo who guards the Water, the Four-Legged Buffalo is there.

The Wily Coyote who tries to take us another way, the Wily Coyote is there.

The Diligent Worm who turns everything over to start again, the Diligent Worm is there.

The Forgotten Soldier of many wars, the Forgotten Soldier is there.

The Flowercup Woman who sends the birds in spring, the Flowercup Woman is there.

The Scolding Boy who keeps bad spirits away, the Scolding Boy is there.

The Singing Girl whose voice attracts the bees, the Singing Girl is there.

Next year's blossoms are there and rain that is yet to fall.

Next year's wars are there and hunger that is yet to come.

A moment of peace is there and a hope that is yet to appear.

The sun pollen is there and dust from the falling moon.

An egg, a root, a bone, and a corn tassle are also there.

Much more is there. You have only to open your eyes to see something new in it each day.

The Old Man held out the Thread to them so they might examine it more closely.

It would made a good souvenir, the New People said, and ran their fingers over the beautiful red blanket that he wore. Is your blanket for sale?

The Old Man saw it was no use to talk to those people. He took the Thread and wound it around himself and went into the plaza. It was filled with the Old Man's people and the New People and some of the Old People from other villages which had not been devoured yet. The Old Man did not care who they were for he had so much to say. The things inside him were ready to come out.

You see, the Old Man said, turning his face to some children, we are of the same material. We came from the same place and we are going to another place together. I am ready to travel with you.

He held out the Thread as a means of transportation. Climb on, he said.

The children laughed and picked up stones and threw them at him until he ran in the strange way he had, limping and leaning to one side. He stopped to catch his breath. All around him, the crowd moved through the heat and the dust, waiting for the dances to begin.

The Old Man looked after them and drew his red blanket around his shoulders, gripping the edge of it with a hand that was knotted like the stump of a tree. His fingers were strong and firm and as brown as the earth he walked upon.

He moved slowly among the people, asking for a Match, saying, a Match is the smallest sort of flame. A Match is a true beginning. With a Match you will be able to find many things. You will be able to find your way in the dark.

But the people laughed at him and said, you're crazy. Go away, Old Man. Go away.

The sight of him made the people shudder and say among themselves, something should be done about people like that.

Yes, something should be done.

Before it's too late, something should be done.

What have I done? the Old Man asked.

They turned away and would not speak to him.

You, said the Old Man, touching the sleeve of a man in a plaid shirt. Would you like to learn a song?

Don't bother me, said the man.

The Old Man let him go and said to another, come sit with me awhile. We will go inside the fire. We need only a Match to begin.

Too hot for a fire, the man said. What we need is rain.

No, the Old Man said, we need clouds before the rain. We need to know the shape and life of rain before it comes.

They did not understand him at all. They drew away quickly, before the Old Man could say any more.

The sun beat down out of a hard blue sky and the clouds rolled in from the west. The Old Man looked up and saw an old buffalo and a young deer he had not seen for a long time. He called his greeting to them, noticing that a great warrior was arriving from the south, followed by an eagle with double wings.

The Old Man saw the shape and life of rain on its way to somewhere else.

We must pray for rain, the Old Man said. We must dance for rain.

In his heart he was dancing and the earth rolled out from his feet and became the music he needed to dance to.

All of my life is a dance, the Old Man said, dancing as hard as he could. But still, the rain continued on its way to somewhere else. Even the old buffalo hurried away and the Old Man prayed for his return.

Next time, the Old Man said, everyone will be dancing. Then the rain will come.

To the east the Mountain rose in the shape it had finally taken which was not the shape he first knew. He stopped and looked at it, remembering when they were both young and being formed.

The Old Man understood the Mountain because he himself was also the Mountain. He had the nature of the Mountain along with everything else he had ever been. He had been rained on a good many years and the winds had blown over him, chiseling out pockets in his rocklike surface. The rain and the wind had formed his features and the snow had cracked his outer layers and run into them. He was formed by the elements and was not finished yet nor would he be because he was infinite under the sun.

The Mountain looked out over everything and saw the red land rising and falling, caught finally by the sky a long way out where the two came together in the place of the Seam. The land and the sky were inseparable. The Mountain saw that the blue sky was part of the red land and that the red land was part of the blue sky. Everything was of the same substance and nature for all were made by One Hand.

Everything is one, the Old Man cried, unable to contain his thoughts in one place, not perceiving the imitation he formed with words.

He picked up a Match from the ground, glad that he had found one at long last. He scraped it against a metal rubbish can. Now is yesterday. Yesterday is traveling to meet tomorrow. All time is one.

The Match went out quickly because there was no one to believe in it.

Come, the Old Man said to the people. I will show you what life is all about. I will leave my body and go with you. Where we go does not matter. Nor when nor how. You must make a choice to travel with the Thread or to travel by yourself.

The Thread spun out away from him, making a rug for the people to sit on. The Thread shone brightly in the sun but the people did not notice it at all. They talked so much that their eyes went dim. They saw each other's lips in motion.

The Old Man spoke to the people in all the voices he knew but still they went on talking among themselves, waiting for the dances to begin. Their automobiles were lined up in the fields around the village. The automobiles sank out of sight as he looked at them and fresh green grass covered the place where they had been.

There is a trick to seeing, the Old Man said. You may see anything you like at any time. You may know the nature of anything once you have experienced it. It is all very simple if you would like to go.

There were three women with the same face, talking together in the same voice, wearing the same pair of shoes. They smiled at the Old Man and asked if he had anything to sell.

Every life is here, he said. Even what is to come. There are certain signs which I will tell you about. He extended his arm from under his red blanket.

The women pushed him away and avoided his eyes which were black and burning. They looked around for their same husbands to protect them. You can't scare us, the women said, and walked away, talking of the same souvenirs, mistaking their rudeness for rights.

The Old Man shrugged and moved on. Up on the platform, a man in a gray suit was addressing the crowd, speaking of the progress the government had brought to the village. On one side of him was a priest who was to talk of the good the church had done for the People of the Sun House Moon. On the other side was a man from a big company which was trying to buy their land; he would talk of the money the people would have if they sold the land they always had.

The man in the gray suit spoke in a loud voice because he assumed the People of the Sun House Moon would understand him better if he shouted. He said what everyone wanted to hear and since they heard nothing, they applauded. The man smiled and sat down and the priest got up and waved one hand up and down, giving a blessing to the people.

Above him, a flag fluttered. The music came out of a box attached to the back of a truck. Everyone stood and sang to what was called the national anthem, looking at the flag with one hand resting over the heart.

But the People of the Sun House Moon left their hands

at their sides. They turned to the Mountain as the priest spoke and listened to the voice of the Rock instead.

Let the earth come into you.

Let your blood become a river flowing with new life.

Let there be a mountain that is strong.

Let there be the growth of trees.

Let there be the beauty of flowers.

Let there be the power of rain.

Let there be one footstep going on.

The People of the Sun House Moon heard what the Rock said and began to dance, harder than ever because of the strength the Rock had given them. The drums, too, picked up the rhythm of the Rock and played such an affirmation back to it that the echo was lost in between and became a melody all its own, rising out and over the land.

THE FOUR THINGS
THAT ARE HEARD

The Old Man turned toward the earth house where he was born and still lived, guarding the Fire and keeping the Spirit of the Corn. On the roof he saw his Ancestors and he spoke easily to them although they were some distance away.

I am still traveling, the Old Man said. I am looking for my destination.

Destination is not important, his Ancestors said. Destination is an end. And an end must have a beginning.

What beginning? the Old Man asked.

The true end, his Ancestors said. The end which comes of beginning.

The Old Man shook his head. His Ancestors always spoke to him in words he did not understand. If the beginning is the end and the end is the beginning, what is in between?

Nothing and everything, his Ancestors said. It is up to you to find out.

I have experienced a beginning which was a point of departure and an end which was an arrival, the Old Man said. I have experienced a lifetime in between.

You have only experienced your own ideas, his Ancestors said. So you have no true power.

Give me this power then, the Old Man said for he desired power greatly.

The true power is the power you already have, his Ancestors said. Go and find it in yourself.

But the Old Man did not know how to go about it.

Life is difficult here, he said.

Life is difficult everywhere, his Ancestors said. Difficulty is part of the lesson.

I am tired of waiting, the Old Man said. Put an end to my waiting. The Old Man was anxious to have things happen.

You must get used to waiting, his Ancestors said. It is in waiting that time passes but time does not pass because of waiting. Time passes because the waiting passes. Pretty soon, you are not aware of it at all.

The Old Man saw that his Ancestors had been waiting a long time and were not harmed by it. One of them flew over the mountains while he waited and learned to fly better. Another leapt through a grassy meadow and learned to run faster. Another swam down through a clear and tumbling river and saw a way to swim more strongly. Another dug a new home for himself in the earth, turning over the soil so new plants could grow more easily.

The Old Man saw that waiting was the only thing they could do. He saw that they were waiting to go from one world into another world. Some of them slept, waiting for the sun to ripen their seeds. Some of them built a cocoon, waiting for a new season to come. Some of them were storing up food and some were drying meat and grain. He saw, too, that some of them had not yet become visible in the nighttime sky for their waiting was of the eternal kind.

But the Old Man saw something else, too.

He saw the fish lying belly up to the sky.

He saw the night bird moving about in the day.

He saw the snake slide out of its skin.

He saw the deer fall from the grass it had just eaten.

He saw the river turn crimson before it turned to dust.

The voice of his Ancestors said, this is what is to come but certain people will be saved. These are the people who have sacred knowledge about the way of the earth. It is the True Way and will last forever.

The Old Man grew exceedingly afraid for the prophecy of his Ancestors came into his vision then and grew more terrible still, with the oceans all on fire and the land bare of every living thing. The Old Man saw the People of the Sun House Moon leave the earth with the other human beings who had learned the True Way. But he could not see where they were going.

The Old Man covered his eyes and cried, I have tried to teach to them what you have taught to me. I have tried to be heard.

His Ancestors laughed and rebuked him.

Only Four Things are ever heard, they said. The Rock. The Water. The Wind. And the Fire. They are heard because the Great Spirit speaks through them.

The Old Man turned around to speak to his Ancestors again but they were gone. Standing on the roof of the house where he had been born were six clowns. They were almost naked except for the cornstalks they wore around their waists. Their faces were streaked with paint they had made from roots and berries. They had branches of aspen in their hair and bells around their ankles. They laughed as they chased the children across the roof. The children screamed as they were carried off.

The clowns said, we will eat you.

But of course they did not. They only threw the children in the clear, cold stream which ran down from the Mountain and through the village. The People of the Sun House Moon washed and cooked and bathed in the stream and went to sleep to the rhythm of its song. The nature of the stream belonged to some of them and to some of them it did not. The ones who perceived the nature of the stream woke up first in the winter when the ice began to break and something deep inside themselves broke also. The ones who did not perceive the nature of the stream had to wait. The nature of something else told them when spring was coming.

The Old Man continued to move through the crowd, searching for a Match so that he could make the beginning he needed in order to find the way to a certain end which was upon him.

The New People pushed and shoved him to get a better view of the dance which was going on. They were hot and tired from the long wait in the blazing sun and they stood on one foot and then the other, wondering why they had come. The dust had settled over them; it had settled in the palms of their hands. They thought about washing off the dust. They did not think that they held a piece of the earth and were thus attached to it. They thought of it as filth.

I would like to go back, the Old Man said to the people. I would like to journey into the earth itself. There is much to learn. My shadow does not follow me there. Do you wish to take the place of my shadow for the time being?

The drums beat from a place which was close to his own heart for it had the same sound and the same rhythm. He saw that the music had entered the sky for the clouds were coming in again over the mountain; the old buffalo and the bear and the deer were all listening. The music of the sky was the same music that the earth played. It was a universal song.

He spoke to them as the music grew and burst and the air was saturated. He told them everything he knew. He saw it all disappear in the clouds which were racing one another, with the deer beginning to win over the buffalo who was clumsy. The clouds interrupted his vision so that he could no longer look out across the land seeing all time as it was. He saw only what he remembered, which was the same thing. His vision had in it a reflection of himself as the Keeper of the Fire and the Spirit of the Corn and the Teller of a Story.

The people pressed together, spilling popcorn and colored soda. In the dancing feet they saw what they had come to see, which was no more than the dance itself; they saw what they believed history was all about.

I have a story, the Old Man said to them. Come to my Fire and listen. Come, for I am obliged to pass it on to you.

It is your end to pass it on, his Ancestors said. Keep your story to yourself if you do not want them to destroy you.

The Old Man hurried faster now for there was so little time left.

Please, he said, I must have a Match in order to create a flame. There must be Illumination from the beginning.

The beginning is the end, his Ancestors said.

But the Old Man turned away from them, remembering the Thread.

Here, the Old Man said, pulling it down and holding it out to the people. Here is the True Way to begin.

It is the true end, his Ancestors said. The true end is when the people accept the Thread.

The Thread carried only the most lasting thoughts from one time to another time and connected all time together and made generation important. The Thread was progress of a certain kind and yet it was the enemy of what progress usually meant. The Thread took mankind into history and yet the Thread left them far behind. The Thread needed each man's story to keep it always reaching out and yet it needed not a word. The Thread was narrow and fragile just as it was wide and strong. The Thread was invisible just as it was plain to see.

The Thread was spun out of the Old Man's eyes.

I must be going, the Old Man said, drawing the Thread around him. There is much to see and much to tell. Everything is in the Thread. You may stand and watch or you may come with me. It is the last time I am going to ask.

The Old Man touched the sleeve of a Straw Man, who drew his arm away and said, can't you see we are watching the dance?

There is a larger dance, the Old Man said.

Up on the Mountain he saw the Wind dancing with a Cloud; he saw Water dancing with Mist; he saw the Rock dancing with Smoke; he saw Fire dancing with Dust. He saw Sky and Earth intertwined with Dust and Rain which was their dance to one another.

We are the Four Things That Are Heard, said the Wind, the Water, the Rock, and the Fire. We will be listened to.

Yes, his Ancestors said. You will be listened to for your voice is everlasting. Your life is the life of the universe. In you, the Earth turns back to itself.

No, the Old Man said. It is I who will be listened to. And he tried to wrap the Thread around the Straw Man.

You are not in touch with the River, his Ancestors said. You are not in touch with the Mountain. You are with yourself too much.

The Old Man was not listening. He was waiting to see whether he would be heard or not.

The Straw Man looked up at the Thread which was just above his head.

A butterfly, the Straw Man said and reached out his hand toward it.

Hurry, and take the Thread, said the Old Man. There is no time to lose.

What would I do with a butterfly? the Straw Man said and turned his radio on and held it to his ear. The rhythm was upside down. It was at odds with the dance that was going on.

The Straw Man said, I am busy. Go and leave me alone.

He turned the radio louder, causing the Old Man to shrink away.

The Old Man saw that everyone on the earth was busy as a form of distraction. He saw them busy as something to do.

He saw that there was no end to such busyness because it perpetuated itself. He looked out at it from the mountaintop through the eyes of the Mountain. He saw that there was no quietness to the moment; it was filled with solid busyness which blocked out sound and allowed only noise. There was no way for a word to be heard above it. There was no way for quietness to enter the moment of mankind. They were always too busy filling up the time.

They do not want to listen, the Old Man cried to the

Mountain where he saw his Ancestors resting on the very top, saying, only Four Things are ever heard. We will show you the way it is.

One of his Ancestors was flying in a great circle, covering up the sun with his wings. He said, they have no use for you. Do you know what will happen if you persist?

There was laughter surrounding the Bird.

The laughter of the Bird was so shrill that it echoed all across the land and was heard as the edge of the North Wind.

All over the land, the people were frightened when they heard the North Wind howling at night and shaking the houses they lived in. They looked up at the sky and wondered where such a wind was coming from; they could not sleep because of the howling Wind of the North. Everything which was not held fast blew off into the night and was not seen again. The people had to start all over because of what the North Wind had done.

The people built new houses out of the wreckage of the old. They made them stronger than before.

One of his Ancestors was a Deer finding new grass under the dry cover of the season. He said, they are content to be as they are. Why must you try and change them?

There was a cry surrounding the Deer.

The cry of the Deer went out over the earth and was heard as the broken pulse of the Rock. The earth split open and the Rock came forth in ways which were hot and liquid. The people ran from the Rock and the Rock pursued them and crushed the places where they lived. The Rock claimed the land and the people had no power to hold it back. They could only listen to the awesome sound of it, breaking and falling everywhere. The Rock was without mercy and the people waited for the Rock to calm down.

As they waited the people began to see the possibilities around them. They saw there were many ways to do things. They began to believe in choice.

One of his ancestors was a Fish in the water, nibbling away at a plant which doubled in size every day. He said, they will destroy everything in time. Why must you fight against them?

There was a song surrounding the Fish.

The song of the Fish rose and fell and rose again in a roar that was heard as the crest of Water. The Water swept away from its course like the wings of a deadly bird, enfolding the raw sore earth. The people stood at the edge of the earth waiting for the Water to recede. They clung to one another and shivered in the cold. The people touched one another for the first time. When the Water ended, the people listened for it again. They went on listening to the Water even when a snowflake was all they heard.

They went on touching one another when they were afraid. They felt the heartbeats of one another. They began to have breath for the first time.

One of his ancestors was a Worm pulling himself along, in and out of the earth, turning it over as he went. He said, how can you turn away from them? How can you forget they are living and dying just the same as you?

There was a whisper surrounding the Worm.

The whisper of the Worm was very soft at first so that no one heard it at all. Then the air committed itself to the whisper and it grew and grew and was heard as the tongue of Fire. The people feared the Fire more than they feared the Wind or the Rock or the Water; the Fire created in them an outline of themselves, filled it in, and devoured it. The Fire summoned the shreds of their beginning and allowed them but a glimpse into something that was strange and wonderful. As the Fire burned, the people could not stay away from it for fear it would go out.

The people wanted more than just a glimpse. They wanted to know what the life of the Fire was all about.

The Old Man gave thanks to the Four Things That Are Heard, understanding the reason for their voices which was the same reason that he himself possessed.

The Old Man hurried away from the Mountain and began to move through the crowd again. The dance was finished now and the New People were walking toward their cars, carrying their souvenirs.

The Old Man had been given new strength by the Four Things That Are Heard and so he said, I have seen a bird turn into Wind and a deer turn into Rock. I have seen a fish turn into Water and a worm turn into Fire. Wonderful things can happen because of it. A Match is the only way to find out.

But the New People were just as busy as they had been before. Nothing had changed in them at all. They looked at the Old Man and said, we want to take your picture. Stand still a minute.

They handed him a dollar for standing still.

The Old Man hopped about in the dust, on his good leg first because it did not hurt him as much as the one which was lame. The Old Man burst into song. The New People who were taking pictures of him took some more, saying, these people are crazy.

But all the same they began to feel uneasy, looking through their cameras at his face.

We should leave before something happens, they said.

The Old Man grabbed the Thread which was drifting off in the wind. He said, I can show you the way life should be in our minds.

No time, the people said.

There is always time, the Old Man said. And he sat down with the Thread which was getting very heavy.

They said, we're hungry, Old Man. We must go and eat.

I will fill you with thoughts, the Old Man said. Then you will not be hungry any more. All I need is a Match.

The people took all the matches they had and threw them on the ground and turned their backs to him. They hurried to their cars and drove around and around, trying to get out. The dust and the smoke obliterated everything except the Thread which the Old Man held on to, drawing the people to him against their will, against all they had come to find out.

How do we get out? the people said angrily. They were afraid to stay any longer in the Old Man's company.

The Old Man said, you cannot get out that way. It is the wrong way. He tucked the Thread into all the cracks and corners so that he had both hands free.

He began to strike the Matches he had found. He struck them one by one. He struck them carefully, trying to preserve the flame.

The people kept driving around and around, frantic to get out. You must help us, they cried. Which way do we go? They began to see the People of the Sun House Moon appearing, making a circle around them.

The Old Man said, I will share the Thread with you. Reach out and pass it to one another. Take hold and do not let go. The Thread is all that lasts.

The people were hot and thristy. Give us some water, they said.

Everything is in the Thread, the Old Man said. Pick it up and drink.

The people were running out of patience. They had not time or tricks. One of them got out of a car and said, here is another dollar. Now, which way is the way out?

The Old Man said, the way out is the way in. The way you are going is the wrong way. You will have to turn around. You will have to find the Thread. The Thread will lead you out.

Another man got out of the car. He said, you have trapped us here. His face was dark with anger. He held a stick in his hands.

Yes, said the first man, you have trapped us here on purpose. What do you want from us?

Nothing, the Old Man cried. I want only to give you a gift more precious than gold.

The people stopped a moment. Where is it? they asked.

The Old Man held out the Thread for the last time. Take it, he said.

But the people saw that there was nothing at all in his hands.

They fell upon the Old Man and knocked him to the ground and hit him with the stick until he no longer moved.

They drove away saying, it was the only thing to do. He was going to kill us. We had to protect ourselves. He was crazy. We did what we had to do.

But they kept on seeing the Old Man's face.

Purification

THE SILVER BIRD
AND THE MOUNTAIN

When daylight came, the Old Man left his body and took the Being of a bird. He wore his beautiful silver wings which were made of light from perpetual dawn solidified into the burning axis upon which the world turned. The Old Man had forged the wings himself, using a hammer made of sun, and the power of the sun was in him as he flew.

The Old Man rose on his beautiful silver wings, far from the earth bathed in a strange golden light. The light formed a curtain which parted to reveal ten thousand wars and ten hundred million dead and a red river spinning around and around until the oceans and the continents were wrapped in a blanket of blood. The anguished cry of the earth echoed throughout the universe, shaking the stars in that part of the sky where it was always night.

The Silver Bird stood out against the red planet, caught in the long and blinding rays of the sun bursting out of the Lower World. The Silver Bird was part of the wars raging below and part of the soldiers who had died and part of the blood surging and intermingling so that it was finally One

War and One Soldier and One Blood and One Purpose undefined.

When he recognized that the purpose of War was never to be defined nor justified nor able to be made into peace, the Silver Bird had pulled the Thread out of all that chaos and had held it ever since. It was for the Silver Bird to know how to fight without killing or hurting; it was for the Silver Bird to know that the power of peace was forever in the Thread.

The emerging sun halted the Silver Bird in his flight and took the outermost tip of his wings and turned them around so the Silver Bird was staring directly into the dark eye of the sun as it howled across the sky: I am the center of life. I am rooted in a sky which has no end. I am the Fire and the Light. I am the giver of life. The earth must receive me this day or else all life shall end.

The Silver Bird, plunging through the dazzling brightness of a new day, opened his mouth and released the Thread because of what the sun had said. The earth began to emerge then from the blanket of blood it always wore at the day's beginning to remind mankind of the dearness of its life.

It is the vision of all visions, the Silver Bird said, watching the Thread encircle the earth just as day began and the sun breathed new life into it. In one form or another, the Silver Bird was always there to prevent the sun's prophecy from coming true. The sun's great dark eye watched the Thread absorb the earth's blood and was satisfied. The sun continued its journey for another day.

The Silver Bird said, the Thread must encircle the earth at dawn or else the sun will reverse itself and go back into the Lower World and stay there forever.

But there was no one to hear him except the descending moon which was hurrying out of the path of the sun. The moon would have preferred an endless night in order to be looked at and admired.

The Silver Bird was carried along by the South Wind which is the Wind Which Awakens and the Wind Which Buries. It is the ultimate wind for it does not settle down but is always moving into the corners of lonely hearts and minds without exhortation; it is the Wind Which Calms and Soothes; it is the Wind Which Shows the Way.

The Silver Bird let the South Wind take him away from the sun, spreading his wings to form a shadow large enough to cover the earth he encircled. The spirit of the Silver Bird with wings made of the sun itself was in the shadow that he sent down and thus it was the shadow of peace which disappeared quickly.

The Silver Bird flew over the Great Sleeping Mountain which was the Mountain of Secrets and Dreams; it was a Mountain which expressed itself in barren rock and lonely streams and treeless space pointing toward a sky which turned the clouds away. The Mountain was so high that even the rain avoided it and its upper reaches were scoured by the Wind Without Direction; it was the Wind Which Comes from Above. It was the Wind Which Comes from the Dark Eye of the Sun.

The Great Sleeping Mountain was home to the Silver Bird and he greeted it with a song. The Silver Bird occupied the space where the notes had been and thus became true music, bursting confinement of form so that what was heard was a true song, possessing the air with the fullest expansion of the note. The Silver Bird was a voice and an instrument both but as his music rose, the voice and the instrument were forgotten. He became the true intention of the song; he became freedom poised on a single note.

The Silver Bird folded his wings and nestled against the Great Sleeping Mountain which was just waking up as he began to close his eyes. He felt warmth coming out of the rock and it was the warmth he remembered from the time before his creation when the face he had was still being formed. It was his Grandmother's face and the time was a half-remembered time which was part of his inheritance already spent. The warmth was related to the fire and to the wings he wore. The warmth was required just as the touch he had forgotten was required. The Silver Bird opened out to the softness and the warmth he perceived the Mountain to have. He absorbed all of the warmth he could for it was deep and nourishing.

The Mountain was still warm from its beginning which was cooling off and turning around inside. The Silver Bird embraced the warmth coming out of the inner universe of the Mountain. He felt renewed and safe pressed into the body of the Mountain which always cured him and took away whatever fear he had. The Silver Bird let himself be drained into the reservoir of the Mountain; he let himself be still even as he was moving, discarding motion for rhythm.

Mankind is about to fall, the Old Man said. I have seen for myself that they are going down.

The Mountain said, if mankind falls, you will fall with it. And I will crumble into dust. Our Essence is too strong in one another.

Mankind does not care, the Old Man said, burying his head in his beautiful silver wings. You may say what you like but they are deaf.

The Old Man had no wish to see anything as it was. He carried with him a vision of what the earth was like before the coming of One Idea. He dwelt within this vision and here defined a life which was not possible. The Old Man perceived the earth to be a reflection of what he saw inside himself for he could not be a reflection of the earth which was too tarnished to form a clear reflection. The Old Man gave the earth an improved image of itself through eyes which accepted only that part of seeing which was in harmony with his vision. All else the Old Man changed as he wanted to.

When he saw a mountain insulted with machines, the Old Man covered it with trees. When he found a field filled with trash, he planted flowers there. The filth of cities he disguised with vertical grass; the metal snarl of highways vanished in the mist he summoned from his eyes. The Old Man wished to see the earth surrounded in beauty; he wished to see it comforted in beauty; he wished to see it safe in beauty. He wished to unify the people with the beauty of a Positive Force.

But this time the Old Man had come with his bitterness. Laying aside the vision which had nourished him for so long, the Old Man was able to see the disrupted moment undisguised. He was able to see where history had dropped its knife and left the wounded earth to die.

The Old Man looked out and saw that the broken pulse of the Rock was already upon mankind. He saw everything in a strange red light and covered with a layer of smoke. He saw that the fields which had been planted were all burned up. He saw that the rivers ran with red dust. He saw that the earth bled red dust through all the pores it had. Because he was of the earth, he felt the pain of the earth. He spoke the same words that the earth did.

Look at what mankind has done, the Old Man said. They have brought destruction upon the earth. They are

chewing upon the flesh of the earth and soon will leave nothing but bone and ash.

The Old Man and the Mountain were one because they
had come from the same source and would return to it, each
in his own time according to his life. The Old Man and the
Mountain shared the earth with one another and had their
common roots. Yet the Old Man and the Mountain did not
always understand one another.

The Mountain said, my experience is different from
yours and yet you know about it because you have worn my
nature and are wearing it still. So what I know, you know.
But I know it differently because there are many layers of
truth. What I know is that mankind will continue to rise.

The Silver Bird which was the Old Man who was part of
the Mountain stretched its wings, covering up the sore land
that lay beneath him. The Silver Bird turned himself around
so that he was headed into the Mountain. The Silver Bird
made himself comfortable and settled down to stay for a
while. He had no desire to see anything more of the earth he
had come from and risen above.

The Silver Bird was the Old Man's sorrow.

Mankind has already fallen, said the Old Man. And it
makes no difference to me. I am comfortable here where I
am. I am going to hide myself in you.

The Mountain had seen the Silver Bird coming and
going in one sort of mood or another; the Silver Bird was
unpredictable and difficult. The Mountain always had to be
teaching the Silver Bird to live up to its nature.

The Mountain said, what have you seen this time?

I? cried the Silver Bird. I have seen all there is to see.
There is nothing more I wish to look at. I am finished with
flying around.

As long as one bird lives, you will continue to fly, the Mountain said. That is freedom, which is the Essence of your nature. You can only pause here awhile and then you must be going, higher than clouds or mountains into the heart of the sky.

I refuse to fly, said the Silver Bird. I am ready to give myself to the earth. Open up and let me come into you.

But the Mountain drew itself tightly together. Even its streams and rivers stopped running and the Wind Without Direction paused, bringing a dead dry heat. Nature was suspended on the Mountain because the Old Man had denied it.

The Mountain was angry with the Silver Bird. The Mountain said, you were singled out a long time ago to give mankind something. What is your gift, Old Man?

But the Old Man only pressed himself closer to the Mountain, enjoying the comfort he had missed. He did not wish to be reminded of all he had been given.

The Mountain said again, what is your gift, Old Man?

The Old Man refused to answer.

Very well, said the Mountain. You will have to start all over again. You will be released from the earth and shall remain homeless until you no longer recognize your own importance. You must possess your solitude before you can have a home.

The Old Man was beyond caring for he was beyond listening; he was beyond reason for he was beyond concern. The Old Man was deep in his own misery.

He shed his clothing and faced the east where the sun held him with its great dark eye. The Old Man raised his arms and released his spirit to be purified; the Old Man sang a song of Purification.

The sun rose higher and higher in the sky and burned through the air, scorching the dry earth even more. The Old Man saw his silver wings begin to melt and the heat of the Mountain caused him to sweat until certain things came into his vision.

First the Old Man saw nothing except the color red which is the First Color of the First Age belonging to the Rock.

Then in the center of the redness he saw the Fire and around that he saw a white light and beyond that he saw Darkness.

The Old Man recognized the Darkness and feared it but Darkness was what he sought because of its coolness and refuge, yet he could not move beyond the tip of the flame which held him. Through the Fire he saw the shape of the Mountain repeated; he saw the Mountain turned inside out, he saw the Mountain red hot and liquid.

The Old Man was terrified for he perceived that he was dying. He perceived that he was not prepared to go from one life into another. At that moment the Old Man did not remember the other deaths he had experienced; he sought only to hold on to what was passing from him. He sought to capture the Essence of his life which was all he had left. He sought to isolate the Essence from the fear which surrounded him.

Then it was that the Old Man remembered the Thread which he had released to the earth in order for the sun to continue on its course. He looked up and saw it hovering over his head and reached up for it, not knowing what else to do. The Old Man reached for the Thread as a tree reaches for the sky or roots reach down into the earth. The Old Man's reaching was part of his nature and he gave no thought to it.

Now that you have accepted the Thread again, you cannot let go of it, the Mountain said. You must take it to mankind and give it to them. Love is the secret of your gift, Old Man. That is why you must keep flying even when it is easier letting go.

And try as he might the Silver Bird could not rid himself of the Thread.

It was your own choice, the Mountain said. You could have left it where it was.

I could not, the Old Man cried. It has always traveled with me ever since the beginning of time.

And it will follow you to the end, the Mountain said. It is the last breath and the first. It is everything in between.

The Mountain moved into the Silver Bird then and revealed its nature to him which was the nature the Silver Bird needed in order to continue to fly. The Silver Bird was consumed by the Mountain and became the energy within it so that it opened fully, exposing all of the layers it had, on down to the core of the earth where the Old Man had to go in order to find the Place of Turning Around.

The Old Man traveled on the Water Running Backwards because it was the path to his roots. The Water Running Backwards was how the Old Man perceived the way in which his nature came into being and the way he had experienced a true end and a true power.

But even as he entered the Water, he forgot all of his experiences.

He entered the Water as nothing but a breath.

JOURNEY INTO THE EARTH
ON WATER RUNNING BACKWARDS

Darkness

The Old Man departed in his nothingness contained in an embryo dead in the womb. It was the nothingness of dark and vagueness confused. It was the nothingness of battle with weapons inscribed in sand. It was the nothingness where greed and promises meet. It was the nothingness of a skull wrapped in an eagle's wing. It was the nothingness by which time travels to meet itself coming back.

The path that the Old Man took was the Path of Water Running Backwards and he gathered it as he went, deeper and deeper, filling his nothingness with the past the water had. He went against the water and the power of the water pulled him away from himself; the flow of the water pulled the Old Man apart for it was his will which took him upward and it was his nature which dragged him down.

The Old Man said nothing for it was against his purpose to speak. All was silence and all was dark; the Water Running Backwards displaced expectation and assumption and ruined all belief. No thought was possible for all was thought and all was without thought. To have thought was to have knowledge of time which had become absent in the strength of its presence.

The Old Man came first into Darkness, which was the First Place of his Purification. In Darkness lay only the memory of Light and it was this memory the Old Man sought as he entered the moist gray edges of Darkness and tried to form a question of its habitat. But no question was possible for no answer was possible. Darkness was by nature silent and undefined; it was unknown and knowing. Darkness was a limitation and yet there was no boundary to it. All was Darkness and the Old Man felt the heaviness of it even though it was without weight.

The Old Man felt the uncertainty of Darkness and the fear that Darkness issued as its obvious property. He felt the wings of a bat brush against his skin. He felt a snake crawl up his leg and push his thighs apart. He felt hands without bodies moving upon his body and there was the uncertainty of intent in their touch. The Old Man stood helplessly in Darkness, having no weapon against it for he would not release memory but cried out to it, using the name of Light.

Now Darkness required only acceptance of it, which was an acceptance of forgetting Light. It was an acceptance of what Darkness offered. The Old Man took a deep breath and expelled it and lost something of himself as it went. Darkness rushed into him then, edging out his memory of Light. The Old Man closed his eyes which held the memory of Light and perceived only Darkness there.

In this way did the Old Man lose his memory of Light. He perceived himself before he was born, living peacefully in Darkness which held no terror for him. The time before he was born included the universe and he found himself there once again; he found himself without definition or intent. He was in a state of pure Being and he began to derive his strength from that.

When the Old Man let go of memory and became one with Darkness, the Darkness immediately departed. The Old Man went through the door that Darkness had made, perceiving he was without Light. He perceived only Illumination which is the true meaning of Light.

Mist

Next the Old Man came to the Second Place of his Purification, which was Mist. He stood at the edge of the Mist, trying to decide the best way to enter it.

He was in a place which offered no assistance and so he stood alone, without conditions or fear. He stood with his curiosity and his temptation to throw himself into whatever Mist contained.

The Old Man began to see certain shapes in the Mist and almost recognized them. They were dark and shadowy and moved slowly, in rhythm with the Mist which was gentle and swirling.

The Old Man said, I have seen such a shadow before. I have seen it pressed into mud and I have seen it sniffing the air.

He began to go in the direction of the shadow but the Mist closed over it just as he put one foot ahead of the other.

Out of the Mist appeared a dark yellow creature with a face that was nearly like his own face, only older and more solemnly defined. It was a face of instinct and survival and the Old Man recognized it as part of his own.

The dark yellow creature looked up out of the Mist at the Old Man and, with a fixed expression of hunger and torment, tried to come where the Old Man was. The jaws of the creature opened and closed with senseless regularity. The jaws were empty and the creature sought to fill them. The eyes of the dark yellow creature were black and void; the eyes were openings through which no recognition passed. The eyes held no history but rather the suggestion of a root.

The Old Man knew the face because he had pondered the skull of it in his hands. He had put his fingers in the openings of the eyes. He had worked the jaws open and shut. He had wondered about the face for he was always looking over his shoulder at it.

The Old Man remained still, watching the dark yellow creature move in and out of the Mist. He watched other creatures too, each more terrible than the last, come and go in Mist.

At last the Old Man said, I am hungry. And he reached out and snatched a fish from the Mist and began to eat. When his hunger was satisfied, the Old Man said, there is food and water here. There is a certain advantage in seeing only partially through Mist. What I see is only Illusion and Imitation. What I see is a past no longer useful except to nourish me for what is to come.

The Old Man lay down where he was, which was neither soft nor hard. He was neither comfortable nor uncomfortable. He had no desire to go on nor did he wish to stay.

I am without a home, the Old Man said but was not sorry for his homelessness. He was at home in Mist which had given him a new perspective of himself. The Old Man went to sleep.

When the Old Man awoke, the Mist had passed over him and in its place was a rainbow with its colors running out, leaving a pale shadow of the earth turned inside out. The

Old Man could see the underside of continents and oceans; he could see cracks in the floor of the earth and the fire struggling to get out.

The Old Man watched what was happening but had no desire to take part in it. He was unable to mourn what was lost for he had overcome loss through placing it in history. It was this history that the Old Man decided to build upon, not for the sake of the history but rather for the sake of generations yet to come.

The Old Man journeyed downward on the Water Running Backwards and yet he had no sensation of descent. He was energy which does not feel of itself. He was energy which expands and illuminates. He was ongoing and invisible in his motion which was not movement; the Old Man was continuous in his journey.

Smoke

The Old Man came next into Smoke, which was the Third Place of his Purification. In Smoke he saw the bones of anger and harshness; in Smoke the Old Man saw every struggle that had ever taken place. He saw a pattern which was irrevocable.

Smoke devours, the Old Man said. Smoke fills up the air. Smoke is the denial of breath. It is the true emptiness.

The Old Man bent toward the Smoke in order to perceive its origin. He saw Fire which had not yet been born but awaited air to give it life; he saw a strange orange light and reached out toward it, anticipating warmth.

The orange light moved away as he went toward it. The light was Fire awaiting birth and the Old Man was not entitled to it.

He was surrounded by Smoke which filled his eyes and

made him blind. It went into his mouth and claimed the air he breathed. Smoke made the Old Man begin to sweat and all the water that was in him ran out through his pores. The Old Man became as dry as a leaf in autumn; he became the hollow shell of an insect which has departed from its life. He could not walk for his legs were stalks of grass and they shriveled away in Smoke. He reached out and grasped the Smoke which surrounded him. The Old Man was still for there was no form or motion to him.

The Old Man was drawn into Smoke which drove consideration from him. Smoke was the basis upon which he was defined but his definition was without form.

A Black Hooded Horse stood in the center of the Smoke; a white flame came from the heavy cloth around his nostrils and blood flowed from the opening cut out in his mouth. The eyes of the Black Hooded Horse were two fiery planets which had not come into being yet and they smoldered through the cloth. A Giant Warrior carrying Fire climbed on the Black Hooded Horse and rode him in and out of Smoke, destroying the places where the people lived.

The Giant Warrior had the head of a bird with teeth like a wolf. He had no legs but rather talons which were long and sharp. He had no arms but rather two enormous wings which lay over the people and suffocated them. The Giant Warrior threw his Fire at the earth and burned it.

The Giant Warrior looked down at the Old Man who was small and insignificant before him. The Giant Warrior's voice was a thunderclap and it was caused by the look in his eye which was lightning. The Giant Warrior and the Black Hooded Horse turned to devour the Old Man with Fire.

There was nothing to protect the Old Man from the Giant Warrior and the Black Hooded Horse except the will he had. There was nothing he could use for a weapon except his spirit which was all he had left of himself.

The spirit was strong in the Old Man and it was the result of mankind having lived. The spirit was indestructible and was an accumulation of all that had ever happened. The spirit was the only weapon that could defeat the Giant Warrior and the Black Hooded Horse.

The spirit was the Old Man's understanding of the Positive Force.

First, the Old Man gave away the only thing he had of value, which was his beautiful red blanket. He was not afraid of losing the red blanket because he had his skin and his skin contained him. He was at home in his skin and thus he was at home in the universe. The Old Man's blanket had been a language speaking in the Old Man's behalf; now the Old Man was forced to speak alone.

I have nothing now, the Old Man cried. I am completely naked.

The Black Hooded Horse lost his first leg because the Old Man had won the First Condition which kept the Smoke alive. The Old Man had given up the only possession that he had.

The Black Hooded Horse and the Giant Warrior were angry at the Old Man and set out once again to devour him with Fire.

The Old Man saw that the places where the people lived were all in flames; he saw the people being consumed by Fire; he saw them raise their arms to embrace what was not there. The people were a long way off, across an abyss growing wider all the time.

The people called to him, we are in great need, good man. If you save us we will give you great reward.

I ask no reward, the Old Man cried. I will help you because you are in need.

And he made a bridge of himself for the people to walk upon. When the people came out of the flame and were safe, they forgot to thank him. They were concerned with finding a new place to live.

The Black Hooded Horse lost his second leg because the Old Man had won the Second Condition which kept the Smoke alive. The Old Man had recognized the Need of Others.

By now the Black Hooded Horse and the Giant Warrior were filled with such fury that the Black Hooded Horse tried to reach him with the flame which roared from his nostrils and the Giant Warrior tried to suffocate him with his wing. But the Old Man was just beyond reach; he was at the edge of Smoke. The Giant Warrior's voice rolled out as thunder which deafened and terrified.

The Giant Warrior said, now you will die.

The Old Man saw that the Giant Warrior had his wing set to suffocate him. He saw that his talons were ready to rip him to shreds. He saw that the fire from the Giant Warrior and the Black Hooded Horse would consume him at the end.

I have nothing, the Old Man said. My life is not important.

The Black Hooded Horse lost his third leg because the Old Man had won the Third Condition which kept the Smoke alive. The Old Man was not afraid of losing whatever life he had. The Old Man had forgotten how much he loved himself.

The Black Hooded Horse was held up by one leg now and the Giant Warrior was having a hard time staying on. He swayed in Smoke and was choked by it. The Giant Warrior laughed and said, you are a member of mankind. Therefore you seek power over the earth. I can give you that power because all power abides in me.

The Old Man stood where he was. How long shall it last? he asked.

The Giant Warrior said, forever.

The Old Man said, how great shall it be?

The Giant Warrior said, greater than the Great Spirit.

The Old Man said, why should you give it to me?

The Giant Warrior said, you have been chosen to have power over the earth.

I do not wish to have power over the earth, the Old Man said. I wish to be what I am, alone and without power. I wish only to unify the people with a Positive Force.

Then the Black Hooded Horse went down because he lost the last leg he had. He went down with the Giant Warrior on top of him and through the Smoke all the Old Man saw was lightning with two forks. The Old Man had won the Fourth Condition which kept the Smoke alive. He had not sought power over the earth.

With nothing to keep it alive the Smoke vanished and the Old Man saw ashes and bone scattered about a hollow field. He saw that Smoke had left Illusion in its place. It was Illusion that the people of the earth had. The Old Man could see that the Four Conditions of the Smoke would destroy Illusion unless Illusion destroyed Smoke. He saw the Black Hooded Horse standing in the shadow of Illusion, waiting for Smoke to catch up.

What must I do to keep Smoke from coming back? the Old Man cried.

Sacrifice yourself, the Giant Warrior said. The Old Man

could see him standing at the edge of Illusion also, coaxing Smoke out into the open.

But the Old Man perceived he had sacrified himself already.

Not for the sake of Illusion, the Old Man said.

The Giant Warrior and the Black Hooded Horse stepped back into Smoke where they belonged and left Illusion on its own.

I am alone in my nothingness, the Old Man cried.

I am without beginning or end.

Essence was all that remained within the Old Man's being and he heard a voice within it saying, give up possession then.

I possess nothing, the Old Man said.

Take no action, the voice said.

I am still, the Old Man said.

Be one with nature, the voice said.

I am a root, the Old Man said. I am my own beginning.

He turned and saw Smoke covering up Illusion.

In his nothingness he passed through Smoke and was not affected by it for he understood the reason for Smoke and with his understanding, Smoke departed. The Old Man gave himself up to wherever he was going, for his will was all that remained in him.

Dust

The Old Man came at last to the center of the earth, drawn back into it on the water which stopped and left him there. The water dried up, going into a small hole, which was the point it had started from. The Old Man tried to go after it since he had no substance but the hole denied him.

All around him was Dust and Dust kept trying to form into something. Dust existed in a vacuum, so it could not be anything or go anywhere but it kept on trying all the same for Dust was the first power of Death. Dust was the Fourth Place of his Purification.

The Old Man stood in the middle of Dust trying to see; in the strange eternal twilight he perceived nothing at all. He had come as far as he could but he could not see through Dust to the Place of Turning Around; he could not find the passage out. The Old Man did not bring light with him nor did he bring air. He had come as he was, alone and without power. The Old Man was without breath; he was without life.

It was neither cold nor hot where the Old Man was; it was neither light nor dark. In his heart the Old Man had always carried a certain rhythm, but now the rhythm was still and the Old Man heard nothing at all.

In the eye of his mind the Old Man had always carried pictures but now his memory was empty. Color had gone from his vision and left a rising gray pressing upon his eyes. The Old Man was always able to taste the sweet fruit of summer and to keep his mouth moist with the rivers of his dreams; now he tasted the dryness of Dust. The Old Man had gone beyond fear for he had gone beyond life and no emotion was available to him.

The Old Man was alone in the nothingness he had become.

He had reached the end of his journey into earth. He waited to be born again, not perceiving the way to be born for thought and memory were dead in him.

But between the Old Man's fingers was a small seed he had brought with him and it fell into the Dust he waited in.

The seed was nourished by the Old Man's tears which sprang from his eyes and kept on flowing. The seed took root and sought the light which came from the Old Man's eyes; it was the only light there was. The Old Man gave his spirit to the seed and a tree began to grow out of it. It was the Tree Which Stands by Itself.

The tree grew slowly and the Old Man perceived that the tree was the only way out of the center of the earth. The tree grew wider as it grew taller and the Old Man grew along with it for he was of the substance and nature of the tree.

The trunk of the Tree Which Stands by Itself was a pillar coming down from the sky. It was the navel of the earth and the opening into the universe. The branches were the first thing that ever grew upward and the leaves were the first green color which is the color of living. The leaves unfolded each time there was someone who believed in them. The branches grew each time there was someone asking for a path to understanding. The trunk thickened each time there was a reason for expansion. The tree took a very long time to grow and the Old Man was patient with it.

Because the tree originated in the center of the earth, it had a long way to go to reach the sun. The Old Man's progress was thus eternal; he could not move unless the tree grew and the tree grew only through the Old Man's belief in its power to do so. The tree did not stop growing and the Old Man continued along with it. The tree and the Old Man grew to where water came out of its hole and they saw that the water was running forward. The tree and the Old Man accepted the direction and nourishment of water and yielded to its power. The Old Man perceived the depth of water, for his energy was in contact with it.

JOURNEY INTO THE SKY
ON THE HOMELESS WIND

When he was born into the earth with the Tree Which Stands by Itself and began to grow with it, the Old Man perceived the Mountain again. He perceived it from the position of standing still; he perceived it from the condition of patience and endurance; he perceived it through a Positive Force.

At last the Old Man was able to draw away from the Tree Which Stands by Itself and to stand in its shadow which gave him the spirit of the tree forevermore.

The Old Man said to the Mountain, I am purified.

But not pure, the Mountain said.

I have gone into the earth and out again, the Old Man said. I have experienced the Four Places of Purification. I have fought with demons and cast them out. Now I know that nothing touches me except the earth itself.

Your journey is incomplete, the Mountain said. You have experienced only half of yourself which is the half connected to earth. You have not experienced the half which is connected to the sky. Nature is made of both.

The Old Man looked at himself and saw it was true. He saw that his own shadow was not yet fully formed for his spirit was incomplete. The Old Man wanted to be in touch with sky as well as earth in order for his shadow to be whole. He saw that it was up to him to decide whether or not to go to the World of the Sky on the wind the Mountain offered which which was the Homeless Wind; it was the Wind of All Directions. It was the Wind Which Required Choice.

So once again the Old Man took the Being of the bird with silver wings and began to pull away from the World of the Earth; he began to see its limitations less and less. He rose so high above the earth that he forgot the wounds the New People had given to it; he forgot the importance of the story that he had and the importance of Fire and corn. The Old Man was able to see that life proceeded whether he was there or not. He was able to see a larger order than what his village in the sun contained and a stronger purpose than carving his story in stone. The Old Man was able to give himself to the Second World of Being which asked nothing of him except that he leave himself behind.

When the Old Man was in his being as a Silver Bird, he remained in the World of the Sky. He was free from the earth and so he was without responsibility for the earth. He was without the roots the earth had given him and so he was able to experience the sky without preconception.

The Old Man roamed the sky with his eyes fixed on the magnitude of what surrounded him. From where he was, he could see the movement of the planets. He could see that the sun never left the sky but commanded it, casting out certain stars and giving birth to others. From where he was, he could see the smallness of the earth below.

The Old Man said, out here the earth's concerns are like

crumbs on a table. The wind will blow them away. What does it matter if there is this year's war or next year's government? What does it matter who wins? What does it matter who loses? The earth is in control of itself. The people will never control it. From here the earth looks like a peaceable place. No desolation lies upon it. If I come too close then I will see the ugliness mankind has given it. How much better to be a bird and leave all ugliness behind.

The Old Man was happy in the World of the Sky where everything was pure and open and free. He could escape the rain by flying away from it; he could avoid the great dark eye of the sun by spreading out his wings; he could find refuge from the night by seeking eternal day.

The Old Man could not land anywhere except on the clouds passing by. He was a prisoner of the sky and yet he was freed by it. There were certain conditions upon which he could return to earth but he had not met them yet. Nor did he care. The Old Man was experiencing a new freedom which his spirit had missed. It was the freedom which was the other half of his purification.

The Old Man rode on the wind in whatever direction it happened to take him. He was alone in the sky and the memory of earth did not interfere with his vision which was open and constantly expanding so that he saw day and night at the same time. The mystery of the sky called to him from the blackness at the end of his vision. It called to him from the light of dead stars and from the remoteness of what had not come into being. The mystery was incomprehensible to him.

The Old Man was afraid to leave the pattern of flight which was his; he was afraid to stretch his wings toward the outer darkness; he was afraid to go too far into what he did not know.

There are limitations in the World of the Sky, the Old Man said, remembering what the Mountain told him.

The Old Man was content to watch the growing and the dying of the moon in a cycle which was fixed and absolute; he watched the turning and yielding of the earth to the sun and he moved out of the way to let it pass. The Old Man sought the company of stars and had the music of the wind to soothe him. He sought the warmth of the sun on days when he felt cold; at other times he was grateful for the shade of the clouds he had come to reason with. He wanted to share his experience with other birds flying by but they always were in a hurry to go somewhere. They always said good-bye to him in voices different from his own.

The Old Man was higher than anything with wings and he was lower than anything fixed in the sky. All was fixed beyond his reach and all was fixed in his memory of Creation which was not a memory at all but was happening every day. Yet there was no day, for the Old Man remained steadily in the light. He could not tell one day from another except when he needed sleep. The Old Man perceived the birth of the universe because of his relationship to it; he perceived that the balance between them was held together by something undefined. It was this balance that was a mystery to him also. He could not form the nature of this mystery into words nor did his thoughts really go together any more.

The Old Man accepted this mystery for he perceived perfection in the sky. He perceived that it was uninterrupted and that it could not be changed by mankind. He perceived that the sky was safe for keeping the spirit which rose to it in hope. He perceived that the sky was the answer to what was impossible on earth.

The Old Man discovered the joy of solitary flight; he

discovered the power of his wings; he discovered silence. The Old Man would have stayed where he was and not returned to the World of the Earth for the World of the Sky was a perfect world. But as his journey went on, the Old Man became aware of his loneliness.

At first the loneliness soothed and comforted him for he was in a pure state of being which allowed no company. It was a state ruined by intrusion; it was a state unable to be shared for there was no common language for it. It was a state in which possibility arose out of isolation and isolation was bred by the exhaustion of effort and idea. The Old Man was content to let things be for it was a Time of Letting Things Be. It was a Time of Rest and Consolation.

But then as the Old Man began to fly closer and closer to the earth to have a look at what was going on, he realized that he missed the touch of the earth beneath his feet. He missed the warmth of his fire in his village made of earth; he missed the People of the Sun House Moon; he missed the argument he always had with people different from his own. He missed the chance to be heard even if he was not heard. He missed his chance to complain.

The Old Man said, I am part of mankind. I am able to perceive the nature of mankind most of all. I am able to perceive the hope that mankind has always had and ruined by its actions. I am able to perceive that it will always be so. I am able to perceive the consolation of trying to create a better world even though a better world is not possible. Only hope is possible and that is the important thing.

The Old Man began to perceive that there was a black cloud which covered the whole earth from beginning to end; he began to perceive it also as an ache in his body which he shared with the bodies of all men. He began to perceive the ache as loneliness.

He saw that loneliness was what separated mankind from one another and that it was what drew them together; it was what they all suffered from and what they knew how to cure least of all; it was a disease of words and yet it was healed by words; it was a condition of isolation and yet it was cured first by isolation; it was a denial of the love of man and yet it was love of a different kind.

In loneliness the Old Man found the Great Spirit present in him. He found all lives living in one space which was the space he himself occupied.

The Old Man saw that loneliness took different forms and gave different occupations. He saw it excused through work and disguised as obligation. He saw it described as a universal condition without a universal conclusion. He saw it everywhere, even in the face of the moon which was the destination of all human loneliness rising from the earth. The expression of the moon was the lonely expression of mankind.

Can I change the face of the moon, the Old Man cried. Can I make it laugh? Can I make it have confidence in itself? Can I introduce it to the sun? Can I interrupt its solitude?

The Old Man saw that he himself was lonely in spite of the sky's fixed inhabitants. He was lonely in spite of the song the wind sang for him and the continuous dance of clouds. He was lonely even when the rainbow gave him color to behold and lightning gave him the benefit of surprise.

The way that loneliness left the Old Man happened in a manner that was appropriate to him.

THE YOUNG BOY
AND THE MAGPIE

Because he had been a Young Boy once, the Old Man had within him the nature of a Young Boy. Because he had been an Old Woman and a Young Girl once, he had in him the nature of an Old Woman and a Young Girl also. Because he was an Old Man too much of the time he had forgotten how to be young; he had forgotten the youth which he once possessed and which was in him still. He had not summoned the Essence which had come out of his youth as wonder. He had forgotten the way in which he had acquired the Thread.

Now as the Silver Bird was soaring high above the earth one day, a change took place in the Old Man. He pulled out of himself his nature as a Young Boy and he looked at the face he had forgotten. The Young Boy's face was full of clarity and question; it was smooth and formless because nothing had happened to give it shape and dimension. The Young Boy's face was one of softness and innocence; it was a face conditioned by what was heard and repeated. It had no individuality of its own.

The Old Man laughed at the sight of himself as a

Young Boy and he had no wish to trade places nor to have his innocence again; he had no wish to have the agility of the Young Boy nor to be at the rim of finding out everything all over again. He was glad he had come to his destination the hard way and that he wore the cost of his experience in his Old Man's face. He was glad that the Young Boy had the choice of going up or down in his own way; he was glad he had his mistakes to look forward to.

That is all I can wish for him, the Old Man said, inviting the Young Boy to climb on the back of the Silver Bird.

The Old Man and the Young Boy flew off together to the east which is the Direction of Understanding; it is the first direction for it is the Direction of the Rising Sun and the Approaching Light.

After a time the Old Man and the Young Boy came to where the Magpie guarded the sun emerging from the Lower World. They saw the Wily Coyote trying to trick the Magpie away from where she stood surrounded by the first light of the new day. The Wily Coyote held a beautiful golden necklace in his teeth.

Come try it on, the Wily Coyote said to the Magpie who was unadorned and plain.

Not I, the Magpie said. Soon I will be covered with light to make even gold seem pale.

The Young Boy saw the way the light consumed the dark; the light kept coming steadily; not even the sky could hold it back nor reverse the direction it was taking.

The Wily Coyote saw the Magpie raise her wing to keep the sun from seeing the world too soon. The Wily Coyote had a house of precious jewels on his head.

Come live in my house, the Wily Coyote said. It is the most beautiful house in the world.

He danced with the house of precious jewels balanced on his head. He wanted to make the Magpie curious. But she did not turn to look at him.

I have a house, the Magpie said. My house is the world. No house is more beautiful than that.

The Coyote began to sing to the Magpie. His tail moved in a beautiful rhythm. His coat sparkled in the sun. Between his feet appeared a huge table of food of every kind.

You must be very hungry, the Wily Coyote said. Come and eat with me. You will be the guest at my table.

The Magpie folded her wings now that the sun was up.

I prefer to eat my own food, she said. The ground was covered with berries and she began to eat them.

The Young Boy looked down at the Wily Coyote trying to trick the Magpie into coming with him. He said, what does the Wily Coyote want with the Magpie?

The Old Man said, the Wily Coyote is cunning but not wise. If he captures the Magpie, he will have wisdom. It is the only thing he lacks.

The Young Boy said, what would the Wily Coyote do with wisdom?

The Old Man said, he would keep it to himself. The Wily Coyote is very selfish. The Magpie has only one duty. To stand between the dark and the light. The Magpie is the sister to the Morning Star and I have known her forever. She is the Holder of the Light.

The Young Boy perceived the Morning Star in the sky; it was she he had been admiring all along. The Morning Star was surrounded by a strange Blue Light.

The Young Boy said, I would like to know the Morning Star because she is the most beautiful star of all. She is fearless and strong.

The Old Man said, what would you do with the Morning Star? She belongs to the sun.

The Young Boy was looking at the beauty of the Morning Star, not seeing the plainness of the Magpie who was stuffing herself with berries now that the Wily Coyote had slunk off.

I would stay with her forever, the Young Boy replied. He could not take his eyes off the Morning Star even though the sun was coming up and blinding him so that he had to turn away from her.

I am in love with the Morning Star and must have her for my wife, the Young Boy said. I must take her away from the sun.

The Old Man laughed for he knew the way everything would turn out. He knew that the Young Boy's love was as burning as the sun which tore a hole in the sky to come through; he knew it was as fleeting as the rainbow trying to paint a bridge from its other side.

The Old Man felt sympathy for the Young Boy remembering the pain he himself had gone through when he saw the beauty of the Morning Star for the first time. The Old Man in the distance of his years had forgotten the closeness of his First Love which was his Last Love also. The Old Man noticed that the Young Boy was just beginning to add the first line to his face because of the pain he was experiencing. It was the line of Desiring.

I will die without her, the Young Boy said, looking back for the Morning Star. But the sun was already up and all he saw was a Magpie standing in a field of berries.

What a silly bird, the Young Boy said. It is not beautiful at all. How can the Wily Coyote want a bird who is so plain?

The Old Man laughed at the Young Boy's foolishness

but said nothing to him. The Old Man took pleasure in remembering the love of the Magpie who was sister to the Morning Star. The love was richer because he remembered it without the details which had come later and spoiled the first experience; the Old Man rejoiced in the freshness that was left and would continue past what was ordinary and tame.

The Young Boy was miserable as he flew along, trying to gain perspective from the position of above. The Young Boy fought against the healing gift of space that the sky was trying to give to him. The Young Boy wanted to go back and search for the Morning Star who had vanished in the sun.

There is nothing to see without her, the Young Boy wept, closing his eyes to everything. There is nothing to see alone.

All that was in his mind was a picture of the Morning Star in all her loveliness, standing between the light and the dark; the Morning Star was what made the Young Boy believe he could match her brilliance; she was what made him believe he could endure.

There is a trick to seeing, the Old Man said. You may see anything you like at any time. You may see a light in the dark.

There is no light, said the Young Boy stubbornly.

Look at the sun, the Old Man said. Is it not warm and enriching?

The sun has turned to blue, the Young Boy said. The sun has died.

Look at the moon, the Old Man said. Is it not cool and refreshing?

The moon has turned to red, the Young Boy said. It is the end of the world. He was ready to drop off the back of the

Silver Bird and fall to the earth alone. The Young Boy was convinced there was no end to his misery.

The Old Man and the Young Boy had seen the land from one end to the other. They had seen the seasons come and go, waiting for a year that spring forgets to come. They had seen the New People moving from east to west and had witnessed what had happened in behalf of progress. They had seen the path that history took across their homeland made of time.

The Old Man was alone in his sadness over what had happened to the earth; he wept for the earth in his heart; he contrived a new earth in his vision. But the Old Man knew that he had to believe that the earth was going on; he had to see the miracle of a seed planted in the dust; he had to see the promise of a Tree Which Stands by Itself. He had to see all that was not there in order to see what was possible to be.

And so he said to the Young Boy, look at the land we have been traveling across. Is it not a beautiful land?

The Young Boy looked down and said, it is a ruined land. There is smoke coming up from the cities. There is smoke coming up from the country. The rivers are running black and there is no place for water to begin.

Look again, the Old Man said. Look beyond the smoke if you can.

The Young Boy was very tired, having traveled with the Old Man for a long time. Everywhere they went, the Old Man asked him the same thing:

Is it not a beautiful land?

Does the sun not shine brightly here?

Are the trees not good and strong?

Is the grass not tall and sweet?

Are the mountains not pure and free?

To everything, the Young Boy answered no. He was tired of the Old Man's questions. He was tired of searching for the Morning Star. He wished to bury his unhappiness in the dark. He had given up on the light.

But he squinted through the smoke coming up from the city which lay below them. He began to see certain shapes and then certain colors diffused in the smoke. He had nearly forgotten what colors looked like because he was so concerned with the smoke. Through the smoke the Young Boy began to see a red circle forming around the city. It was not a continuous circle but was broken at regular intervals.

A Blue Light began to fill up the center of the circle and to run out at the intervals; the Blue Light rose to the sky through the intervals in the circles. It rose through the smoke with such force that it sliced the smoke apart like a knife. Then, as the Young Boy watched, the Blue Light in the center of the red circle got stronger and stronger and changed then into a White Light so intense that it blinded him and melted the fury that he had. The White Light etched another line into his face which was the line of Awareness.

What is the Blue Light? the Young Boy cried. And his heart beat wildly for he thought he had found the Morning Star again.

The Old Man said, something to believe in.

The Young Boy laughed. There is nothing to believe in, he said.

The Old Man said, the light is believed in.

What is the name of the light? the Young Boy asked.

It has no name, the Old Man said. And yet it goes by every name there is. You can call it what you will and it will not matter. The light requires nothing except belief in it.

The Young Boy was puzzled and he turned his face toward the Blue Light and found that it had taken a shape which was reassuring and familiar although he had not seen it before. The Young Boy smiled in anticipation and recognition. The Blue Light seemed natural and warm to the Young Boy and he held out his hands to it for he was cold. But the Blue Light remained where it was because the Young Boy had not gained the acceptance of the Blue Light. It was too soon for him to believe in it.

The Young Boy said, the Blue Light does not seek me out so why should I seek it? I will forget about the Blue Light.

But he found that all he could think about was the Blue Light which formed the substance of the sky.

There is a time for seeing, the Old Man said. There is a time for the Blue Light to remain where it is. There is a time for the Blue Light to come home. Over his shoulder, the Old Man saw the Magpie coming to assume her position as sister to the Morning Star.

The Blue Light finds no home in me, the Young Boy said. But already the Magpie was watching him.

Do you wish a home in the Blue Light? the Old Man asked, seeing the Magpie spread her wings. He saw the Wily Coyote moving near.

Yes, said the Young Boy for there was no other answer.

Then look up, the Old Man said.

The Young Boy saw that there was a Thread floating above them. It was a strong and endless Thread which filled up all the distance the Young Boy had traveled across and was coming to. The Thread was tangled up and twisted and the Thread was even and straight. The Thread was worn thin and strained. The Thread was not able to be broken.

What is it? the Young Boy cried in fear.

The Old Man said, the Blue Light is the substance of the Thread. The Blue Light is there if you wish to see it, and if you do not, you will not see the Thread. The Thread is the beginning and the end. The Thread is all that connects this age to the next and so on forever, just as it has connected all the ages that have ever been.

The Old Man saw that the Magpie had begun to turn herself to the sun.

The Young Boy did not understand the Thread but he could see that it was a continuous stream of light which poured in upon him and burst upon his blood. The Thread was the artery which connected him together. The Thread was what established his singular beat.

The Young Boy perceived it thus which was his own way of perception belonging to no one else. The Young Boy was accepted by the Blue Light because of his interpretation of it. The Young Boy had given the Blue Light his trust. The Magpie waited at his feet, having guarded the sun until it was finally up.

At last the Old Man said, reach out and take the Thread with you.

The Young Boy was afraid to reach out toward the Thread. It seemed a long way off and yet it came to him instantly when he thought about it. The Thread waited for him to touch it. Then it was around him and in him in such a way that he did not see it at all but felt it moving with him.

The Young Boy looked down at the Magpie at his feet and said, the Morning Star has fallen from the sky. She has given up the sun.

He held the Magpie to him and did not let her go. The Young Boy believed he had captured the Morning Star at long last and that she was the light he needed.

I am not alone, he said, warm and at peace with himself.

He and the Old Man began to fly again, out over the land on the West Wind which is the Wind of Growing. Everywhere they went, the Old Man asked him the same thing:

Is it not a beautiful land?

Does the sun not shine brightly here?

Are the trees not good and strong?

Is the grass not sweet and tall?

Are the mountains not pure and free?

To everything, the Young Boy answered yes. He held tightly to the Thread and laughed with the Morning Star.

The White Light rose from the earth and blinded him and in his blindness he saw that all was as it should be in the place where his spirit dwelled which is called the Second World of Being. The Young Boy wished to do one thing however; he wished to see if all was as it should be in the place where his body dwelled which is called the First World of Being.

The Young Boy went down to see about mankind in the First World where they were going about their life.

The people that the Young Boy saw were all busy. They were busy going from one place to the next. They were busy standing still. They were busy deciding what to put on and what to take off. They were busy talking about being busy. It was the way of the First World life.

The Young Boy said, what are you doing?

And they said, we are busy being busy. Can't you see?

He looked at them and saw it was true.

Then the Young Boy said, why are you busy?

And they said, it is the thing to do. Can you think of any other way?

Of course he could but he decided not to tell them.

The Young Boy said, how long have you been busy?

Forever, they said. It is our nature to be eternally busy. If we were not busy the world would not move in our direction.

The Young Boy said, you cannot be busy all of the time. You must stop and look around.

Even when we look around, we are busy, they said. We are busy deciding what to do with what we see.

There is a time for doing nothing, said the Young Boy. There is a time for sitting still.

But the people shouted at him, we cannot get ahead if we are sitting still. We cannot get ahead if we are not busy. Please get out of the way.

Please stop being busy, said the Young Boy. Come and look at the light.

The people laughed at him and went on being busy. We do not care about the light, they said. Light has no substance. Light only helps us to be busy in the dark.

Such light will not help you to see at all, the Young Boy said. It will only blind you in the end.

We see what we want to see, the people said. We see a way to make use of the earth. We see a way to gain control. We do not need light for that.

There was a Young Girl standing among the people being busy. She said to the Young Boy, I am not busy.

Why not? asked the Young Boy.

I have no reason to be, she answered. I have time to look at the light.

The Young Boy and the Young Girl stood in the middle of the people being busy and they looked at the Blue Light together. They saw that it made everything seem beautiful; they saw it lent possibility to perhaps.

The Blue Light filled up the space around them and they followed it through one of the intervals in the circle. When they came out on the other side the Old Man was waiting for them.

The people were all busy, the Young Boy said. They had no time to look at the light. Why does the light continue if people refuse to believe in it?

The Old Man saw that the Young Girl had come with him. She is the Holder of the Light, he said. As long as she holds it, there will be light around the people who are busy. The Blue Light will travel in a Circle and the Circle will be made of the Thread. That way the people always have a choice. They will be reminded of the Second World which is the World of the Thread.

The Young Boy perceived that the Young Girl was the Morning Star and the Magpie and that she guarded and kept the light. He perceived that there was but one nature between them and that it was connected by the Thread.

As he grew in his knowledge, the Young Boy's face began to form and grow deeper; his face took on the Blue Light that the Young Girl gave to him; his face wore the expression of fear and hope which is the twin expression of mankind. The Young Boy was touched by the Young Girl who became part of his nature; she was the half which dreamed. The Young Girl was essential to him for she was of the same substance and nature as all he lived by; she was the reason for rain and the singular flower; she was the mystery unexplained.

The Thread thus became the way in which the Young Boy lived and it was the way in which his innocence died. The Thread was passed to the Young Boy the moment he trusted the light. The Thread was firmly in place and never left him after that.

The World of the Sky was thus established forever. The stars fell from their place and became women. The moon was relieved of its loneliness and there was Illumination everywhere.

Although the Magpie continued to guard the rising sun and the Wily Coyote continued to try and trick her, the Young Boy perceived harmony between them. He perceived they needed one another to balance out.

The question of reality arose for the first time and the Young Boy made his choice which was the choice of the Old Man also. They saw reality unrelated to what was happening in the First World of Being which is the physical world. They saw reality creating a new world within the spirit which is the Second World of Being. It was the world where the Young Boy began to expand as he grew.

Expansion

THUNDER ALONE

The Old Man was quiet within himself for the World of the Sky had given him peace and the Young Boy had opened his eyes to what he thought he had forgotten. The Young Boy had taken the place of his shadow for the time being, reminding him of all that was possible to do. The Old Man was in possession of a structure which enabled him to build. The Old Man was nearly complete.

One day the Old Man flew down to the Mountain and said, I am ready to return to the earth.

Not yet, the Mountain said. You cannot return to the earth for there is no substance to you. You are an outline of yourself. Your strength is an imitation of desire. It is a repetition of what all men crave. Your strength is not strong enough to take spirit out of your shadow.

The Silver Bird turned himself around so that his shadow fell on a crack into which much rain had fallen and into which the wind had blown much earth.

There, the Silver Bird cried. A cornstalk is coming out of the crack. I have the power to make the corn grow. The power is in my shadow. And he watched the corn growing out of the crack in the rock.

He was pleased with himself and stretched his silver wings to impress the Mountain with his power.

The more you are taught the less you learn, the Mountain said and shifted itself ever so slightly so that the crack closed up.

Now do you believe your power is greater than mine? the Mountain said.

The great silver wings folded up and the Old Man dragged himself to a rock and sat down.

Sometimes I am on the right path. Sometimes not. Sometimes I have great power. Sometimes I am weaker than an ant. Sometimes I believe I can change things. Sometimes I believe I cannot. Sometimes I believe I am able to unify the people with a Positive Force. Sometimes I believe I cannot. The trouble is, I have remembered the Old Woman I thought I had forgotten. I am still aware of her Being which was part of my Being as well. The Old Woman is the Yellow Corn Mother. Without her, my crops have failed.

Find the Old Woman then, the Mountain said, and go to the sky with her. Go to a place you have not been before and discover what lies there.

The Old Woman had been separated from the Old Man for a long time and he did not know where to find her; she was gone from him and yet all that she was remained in him. The Old Woman was part of the sky and part of the seasons also. The Old Woman was no longer in the Seam and the Old Man had grown tired of living there without her. The Old Man was bitter in his recollection of all that had once been beautiful and then so unbearable for time in its widest and hardest span. The Old Man was afflicted with a memory that had no cure.

Where shall I go? asked the Old Man who did not know where to begin.

Wherever the Homeless Wind takes you, said the Mountain, for it will be the true place.

The Old Man found himself suspended between earth and sky in a place which was solid and green; it was a place of thick green plants and exquisite flowers and scented water coming out of deep, white-edged pools. The Old Man gasped at the sight of such a place for he had not know such beauty before; he had not known the fragrance which came from the flowers which were as large as trees and as delicate as butterflies; he had not known such warm and soothing water to bathe in.

The Old Man gave himself to the flowers because it was the natural thing to do; he was totally surrounded by fragrance and nothing more; he was the pollen naked between the petals; he was blown out and over the thick, lush land anxious to receive his seed.

The Old Man stood up and wept and his tears formed dew upon the flowers.

The Old Man touched the petals of the flowers and his touch created gentleness.

The Old Man smelled the flowers and his desire created purpose for flowers which are not smelled.

The Old Man looked at the flowers and his vision created presence for flowers which are not seen.

As the Old Man stood back from the flowers, he saw that there was a dewdrop growing larger and larger, shining in the sun with the brilliance of a crystal. He saw that the dewdrop contained a rosy, long-stemmed flower more beautiful than the rest. The flower had the face of the Young Girl in it and the Old Man reached out for her, crying, how beautiful you are.

The moment that the Old Man picked the flower, everything changed.

The green vision turned to brown.

The plants became cornstalks growing upside down.

The dewdrop became a blowing desert.

The Young Girl stood before him as an Old Woman. She held a cactus in her hand.

The Old Woman perceived the Old Man as a butterfly with golden wings. She held out her arms to him. Where are you going? she asked.

The Old Man picked up the Thread which was lying in the dust of the desert. I am going north, he said, deciding on the Direction of Introspection.

All directions are the same to me, the Old Woman said, so it will not matter which way we go.

She climbed on the Old Man's back and took hold of the Thread so she would not fall off and the Old Man recognized her touch which he thought he had forgotten. The Old Woman's laughter was the music they traveled by. Her words drowned the loneliness in him. Her breath made him fly higher and freer than ever.

You are the Old Woman Who Never Dies, the Old Man said. You live in the south and make the crops grow. In the spring you send the birds back. You give blossoms to the trees. You are the woman who holds up half of the sky.

And you, she said, you are the Old Man Who Never Dies. You live in the north and the Spirit of the Corn is in you. When the corn is planted, you visit each seed with your power. When the corn is reaped, you cut the last of it, and bid the earth good rest in winter. You are the man who divides fire in the sky.

The child we had, the Old Man said, he was the Harvest Child. He carried sunlight in his hands.

The child we had, the Old Woman said, she was the Planting Child. She carried raindrops in her hair.

The Old Man and the Old Woman laughed for joy and their laughter rolled across the sky and awakened Thunder which made no reply the way it usually did when the Old Man or Old Woman laughed.

The Old Woman said, let us discover why there is no answer to our laughter. Let us find out what is happening to Thunder.

The Old Man had missed the Old Woman's curiosity and so he went with her to the Place Where Thunder Lives.

Thunder was living by itself because Lightning had left it a long time ago when mankind ceased to believe in anything higher than themselves. When mankind began to fall, Lightning went back to the sun from which it came and remained there unnoticed, leaving Thunder behind. But Thunder belonged with Lightning and tried to find it, having neither voice nor vision to go by. Thunder was left with intuition beside it.

Now since Lightning had been absent for a long time, the substance of Thunder Alone became silence. Thunder Alone grieved in this silence which was so great that the stars, which were used to Thunder shaking the sky, began to go out, one by one. There was a certain absence in the sky which was the absence of Lightning and Thunder together. It was the absence of what ought to be perceived as One.

The Old Woman lay in the substance of Thunder Alone and said, from here looking back I can tell you I am summer. From here looking back I can see myself coming and going. I will come and go forever. I am Mother to the Earth. In me, everything is growing. In me there is no end.

The Old Man lay there with her. He was unable to speak because the substance of Thunder Alone was too much with him; he was unable to speak because he had grieved for the Old Woman that way.

He looked out across a great distance and was drawn across it until there was no distance at all but rather a pattern of experience which became visible to him.

Between the distance and the Old Man was where everything happened. The Old Man could see that the moments of time had achieved a form which rose and fell in a pattern which was always the same.

It was a pattern of living and dying and being born.

It was a pattern without variation or escape.

It was a pattern which could be seen even though everything in it had happened a long time ago and would happen in time to come.

It was a pattern of prediction which was also a pattern of past and the two patterns nullified each other so that only the present remained.

The images of past and prediction were visible; the images were the sole possession of time.

The Old Man marveled at what he saw for he had often wondered where time went. Each moment was an image caught and recorded in the distance ahead and behind but there was no dimension to either. Each time he tried to follow time, he found there was no end. Each time he tried to meet what was to come, he found no beginning at all.

The Old Man was able to perceive what had happened before and what was to happen after. He saw that the future repeated the past because it was of the same substance and nature as the past. He saw that no moment was really new although each moment was made of newness. He saw the moment related to One Way which is the Beginning Way of Creation. It is the Way to which the whole of the pattern is connected. It is the Way with a destination which has no end and an origin without beginning.

The Old Man perceived the summers of the Old Woman and saw a pattern of drought and plenty. He saw a pattern of determination and despair and a repetition of flowers which were not the same flowers but the continuation of the importance of flowers. He saw past and future summers canceling one another out. He saw one eternal summer held where it was in distance distilled from past which gave Illumination to it in the single moment called the present.

The Old Man said, I have perceived you as endless and so you will never die even though you are not with me any more.

The Old Woman laughed and he saw that she was the Young Girl he had loved many times over with whatever nature had been his. With her he had built a nest on a rock ledge in the warmth of a springtime sun. With her he had stood in the forest, looking out in every direction at once for they had grown together as one tall tree. With her he had circled the earth in the sea as two great fish. With her he had given life to a new generation of mankind already dead. With her he had brought rain to corn long harvested. With her he had planted new seed.

Looking out across the distance he saw that it contained a record of every human being born in the World of the Earth and those who were yet to come. He saw too that the

Thread had rolled out across the distance away from him, gathering up the moments in and out of time.

The Old Woman's face was deeper than the Old Man's face for it had the whole yearning of mankind upon it. The Old Woman's face was of perpetuity and new life; it was of continuity and old order. The pulse of all generations was within her body; in her was the promise of spring and so it was an eternal promise. The Old Woman believed in it and everything she looked upon was given the benefit of her immutability.

Thunder Alone yearned to speak to the Old Woman and to gain from her the assurance of the Lightning he lived without. But Thunder Alone could only reveal its substance which was silence and make it echo through the universe. Thunder Alone could only make the Old Woman ache from the weight of its substance which was the weight of all mankind. Thunder Alone perceived mankind bound by a silence so great that it fastened them to emptiness of mind; it exposed them to a pinched horizon and caught experience in narrow doors.

The Old Woman said to Thunder Alone, do not grieve so much for what seems to be lost for I am into life on your behalf. I am there because you cannot be. Your desire is felt by me and so I find myself negotiating your moments along with mine.

Thunder Alone could not speak; it could only mourn for what was lost. Thunder Alone could not recognize the pattern spread out to either half of the sky; it was only able to accept the moment in and out of time, an isolated moment attached to the navel of mankind. Thunder Alone expanded its silence so that the Old Woman could not tolerate being there. She climbed on the Old Man's back and settled in his wings which were warm and deep. She buried her head in his uncertain wisdom and felt whatever strength he perceived.

The Old Man said, if Thunder is reunited with Lightning, you will be reunited with me. The silence of Thunder will disappear and its voice will echo across the sky.

Our unity depends on what we do not possess, the Old Woman said. It depends on the will of the Great Spirit. Our unity is natural and yet it has been denied for a reason unknown. We cannot question it. We can only accept what is.

Looking out at the Thread, the Old Woman saw that Thunder and Lightning were together again although when or where their unity took place was not important.

It is, the Old Woman said. It was. And it will be.

But the Old Man could only see that Thunder was denied in that time. He could only see that Thunder was always alone.

The Old Woman departed from the Old Man then and yet she was in him more than ever.

You are Lightning, the Old Man said but no words were heard; his words could not be heard because the Old Man was without a voice. He was without belief in their eventual unity.

The Old Man recognized himself then.

I am the Thunder Alone.

The Old Man became comfortable with his Silence and found himself in full possession of his solitude. He perceived himself to be always on the edge of an answer; he perceived it to be his reason for going on.

THE MOON-FACED DOG

The Old Man returned to the Seam in a form without definition for he was in his Being as a spirit; he was not seen or
heard nor was expectation placed upon him to be seen or
heard. The Old Man was in the privacy of expansion, owning
nothing except himself nor being owned by the world in
which his body rested. He knew many things and he kept
them to himself for a long time for his Essence was Silence
and Silence commanded him. The Old Man was in a Time of
Keeping Thoughts to Himself. He was in a Time of Awareness which is the hostage of Silence.

Thus it was that the Old Man began to notice the seasons coming and going and perceived a rhythm to them. He
began to notice the substance of the day and the substance of
the night and perceived the balance between them. He began
to perceive an everlasting pattern created by One Hand. The
Old Man began to perceive that there was a common nature
to all living things. He began to perceive that there was a Positive Force behind everything that happened.

All of these thoughts began to work into the Old Man's

consciousness and to stir certain memories which were not memories at all. They were part of the Thread which he always had with him, even when he was becoming purified. As the Old Man's awareness grew, he began to experience a need to share whatever thoughts he had and to place his thoughts in a form that would be recognized and understood. There was nothing else he could do for the Circle of his life was constant and changing. The Circle was the way he traveled through time and the way in which time took him on a passage that was inevitable.

The Old Man perceived that his passage from one part of the Circle to another could happen in a single day or in a moment when he lived and died and was born only to die again. The Old Man struggled to keep his Silence which was his power over himself and yet his words came out for he was unable to keep them back.

The Old Man said, there is a time for being close and a time for keeping away. Sometimes the warmth of a human fire is all that matters. Sometimes the world is on a mountain-top, listening to a storm being born. Sometimes it is in watching a child at play. Sometimes it is in watching a spider spin its thread. Sometimes it is in putting your feet in the ground.

There is a time to speak and a time not to betray the silence. Sometimes laughter opens a door that has been closed too long. Sometimes it is just the sound of the wind in the trees. Sometimes you can hear a leaf opening or a green shoot coming out of the earth. Sometimes there is weeping with someone else. Sometimes there is weeping alone.

There is a time to sit and think and a time not to think at all. Sometimes it is good just to sleep in the sun. Sometimes it is good to forget where you are. Sometimes it is good not to move.

The sound of the Old Man's words went out with the Smoke which was always drifting around his village made of earth and they were heard by the People of the Sun House Moon. The Old Man's words made the people stronger. The Old Man's words kept his Fire going so they could always tell where he was, even in the dark. The Old Man's words made the corn grow better.

The Old Man stayed where he was giving his words to his people who were a People of One Way and the Old Man was of One Way also. The Old Man and his people strengthened one another and gave comfort in winter when it was dark and cold. The Old Man encircled his people with the Thread and the people were glad when they recognized the Thread and became part of it.

But no matter how much the Old Man said to the People of the Sun House Moon, he did not hear Thunder in the sky. He knew it was because he had not gone outside his village with his words. He knew it was because he had not discovered an answer after all.

One day when he was out listening to his corn grow, the Old Man laid down his hoe and wrapped his red blanket around him and set off for the town where the New People lived. As he went along the road, he looked for his Ancestors for he was in need of company. The Old Man saw them on a cloud coming in from the south, moving on a path which was the right path. The Old Man faced south, the direction he always faced, and called his greeting to them.

His Ancestors said, where are you going in such a hurry, with your red blanket wrapped around you? Where are you going without benefit of direction? Who told you to leave your world and go into another world?

The Old Man was impatient to get there but he was obliged to stop in front of his Ancestors and speak. I must go into whatever world there is, the Old Man said.

But his Ancestors only laughed. You'll see what a difficult world it is.

You have great wisdom, the Old Man said. You have lived many lives in different places. What makes you speak so harshly?

We live in the unlived present, his Ancestors said. We carry the past and future with us. We are the serpent which swallowed its own tail. We are continuous and so we can only tell you what we know. The world is always difficult.

I am no longer afraid of difficulty, the Old Man said. I am of positive faith. I am in search of an answer.

His Ancestors laughed again. Then do not speak, they said. Thought is your only power. Do not give it away.

But I must tell mankind a story, the Old Man said, anxious to be going. I must break the silence in them.

I told them a story, said the Deer, and they shot me the moment they heard it.

I told them a story, said the Fish, and they caught me the moment they heard it.

I told them a story, said the Tree, and they cut me down the moment they heard it.

I told them a story also, said the Bird, and they tamed me the moment they heard it.

But when I told them a story, said the First Man Who Ever Was, they listened. I told them the First Story That Was Heard. That is the story you must go on telling.

What story is it? the Old Man asked. That is the story

they will listen to. It is the story that will break the silence in them. It is the story that will provide an answer.

But his Ancestors vanished at that instant and all that was left was a little pile of dust which began to blow in the wind. The Old Man heard the laughter of the wind mocking him but he kept on going because of the things inside him that needed saying and the Thread that was growing heavier all the time.

When the New People saw the Old Man coming toward them, they stopped.

It's you again, they said. What do you want this time?

The Old Man said, look up at the sky and see what is coming in on the afternoon wind. Look at the bear dancing with the jungle cat. Look at the headless serpent and the big-mouthed fish with a worm.

He raised his arm toward the sky but the New People were watching two dogs fighting in the street instead.

The Old Man continued, out here you may see whatever you wish to see at any time and in any place. You can carry the idea with you and set it down and there, you can have a tree coming out of the sidewalk. You can have an eagle ten feet tall.

The New People laughed the way they always did at the Old Man. In town he had been arrested once for craziness and sent to jail. Do you want some wine? they said, because it was the thing to do.

The Old Man shook his head and sat down on the curb which was the only place there was. To him, it did not matter. All places were the same for he carried them in his heart.

The Old Man saw that they were leaning against their automobiles now, ready to get in. They wore expressions that he had seen before on all men who wore suits and spoke from a position which was higher than the people. But the Old Man continued to talk to them anyway.

Are you afraid to look at the sky? he said. Because if you are, you will never see that sooner or later everything is reflected there.

The Deer as he leaps with his legs drawn up, the Deer is reflected there.

The Buffalo who stands in the west and guards the water, the Buffalo is reflected there.

The Coyote who tries to trick the Magpie as she guards the sun in the east, the Coyote is reflected there.

The Bear who keeps looking inwardly at himself in the north, the Bear is reflected there.

And the sacred Dove of the south whose breath gives life to everything, the Dove is reflected there.

They are all in the shape of clouds. Sometimes the Coyote chases the Deer because that is his nature. Sometimes the Magpie pecks at the Dove because that is her nature. Sometimes the Bear teases the Buffalo because that is his nature. All over the sky, the two-legged animals and the four-legged animals are chasing one another and having a good time. Sometimes, too, there is a Fish who behaves as if he were in water. He swims along with his mouth open and all that you see are his bones because he has starved to death. Look up at the sky. There is a fine horse who is being chased by a two-headed bird with wings in the shape of a wave. All sorts of things happen in the sky and you may say they are improbable things. You may say they are only clouds. But they are dancers to the sky and make it laugh. Every moment, the wind is upon them, so they do not last long. The wind is the keeper of the sky's expression and it has no sense of humor.

The people had driven away from the Old Man while he was talking and left him there. All that was left was an old yellow dog. The Old Man saw that it was a Moon-Faced Dog and that it had a tail which wagged in a continuous circle. The Moon-Faced Dog was the color of honey. It followed the Old Man as he went down the road and cast a shadow to the right of him.

The story you told was the wrong story, said the Moon-faced Dog.

What is the right story? asked the Old Man.

But the Moon-Faced Dog only wagged his tail in a continuous circle and said nothing.

After they had gone many miles, the Old Man sat down along the path, in the shade of one tall tree growing toward the sun.

A tree is a very good thing to be, the Old Man said, deciding to tell of his experience as the Tree Which Stands by Itself.

One time long ago in an age that is yet to come, I grew on a mountaintop, looking out in every direction at once. My branches were turned toward the sky, reaching out for the sun passing by. My roots went down into the earth, deeper and deeper, until at last I was able to stand alone. I was able to split the rock where I had been born, just a seed working its way toward the sun.

When I was a tree, I lived inside the universe where I found myself to be. When I was a tree, I completed my Circle, going down as I was coming out, deeper and higher until at last I bent back against myself, connecting root to sky.

The earth and the sky became one, held together by the tree flowing on at either end. I became a definition of time not measured by sleep or condition. I was a continuous definition, moving out and around itself.

I was not lonely as a tree. There were always birds sitting in my branches, singing the sweetest of songs. They built nests in my arms and when their babies hatched out, they brought them worms and insects to eat. The babies learned to fly from my branches and when they fell, I would catch them if I could.

There were squirrels who lived with me and porcupines who came and stayed two weeks. There were butterflies and mosquitoes and moths. There was a carpet of flowers in summer and grass that caught the rain that fell from my leaves. There was a stream nearby which sang to me day and night. When the wind was in my leaves, I sang back to it. All around me were other trees and we nodded back and forth and tried to see who would grow tallest. Sometimes our branches touched and sometimes we grew so close together that it was difficult to tell one from the other.

From where I was, I could always see what was going on. I could see the growing and dying of the moon. I could watch the sun come out of the Lower World and travel across the sky, warming me as it went. I could watch the wandering stars tiptoe across the night and I could see Lightning make a fork for Thunder's tongue.

Rain and snow fell on me and wind shook my branches and pushed against my trunk and took away my leaves in the fall, leaving me naked, clawing away at the sky. There were storms that ripped the branches from my trunk and fire which burned through my bark and ate away at the Circles of my life.

Still, I did not die. My roots were deep and my sap ran through every branch and bled out through my wound and healed it up in time, although I never looked the same again. Sometimes people came and carved on me. Sometimes they tore off my branches for a fire.

The way I died was when they cut me down. I felt the blade of the axe cut through my bark and then through all the Circles that had taken so long to grow and then to the very heart where all my secrets were. The people stood back and watched me trying not to fall but it was no use. They heard me scream and die.

Even then, what was left of my branches and leaves went back into the earth and another tree grew where I had been. My Circle nourished another Circle and that Circle will nourish still another, just as the First Circle nourished me and the Last Circle will be nourished by me. All these Circles are one Circle. The trees are but one tree growing out along the edges of time. They are like spokes in a wheel.

The Old Man looked at the Moon-Faced Dog. That is the way I remember it. Even now the tree always speaks to me. And I am convinced of the tree.

The Moon-Faced Dog was lying down, chewing on a bone that had been dropped in his path.

The story you told was the wrong story, he said.

The Old Man jumped up with a stick in his hands, intending to hit him with it. What is the right story? he cried, and started to swing at the Moon-Faced Dog. But the dog retreated into his shadow and was safe within it.

If I told you the right story, what would you have then? said the Moon-Faced Dog, coming out into the sun. Come, we must be going.

Where are we going? the Old Man asked, hurrying after him for he did not want to be left behind.

The Moon-Faced Dog sniffed the ground and turned himself around and around until he got his direction again.

This way, he said and set off.

But that is the direction we came from, the Old Man complained.

What difference does it make, said the Moon-Faced Dog and began to wag his tail in a continuous circle, drawing the Old Man in.

The Old Man went along until he came to a fork in the road and there he saw the Harvest People in an orchard, picking apples. The Old Man clapped his hands. I will tell them a story about apples, he said. Perhaps that will be the right story.

The Harvest People who were picking apples looked up and waved at the Old Man. They said, we are in a hurry to be finished. Will you help us or not?

Of course, said the Old Man and he went over the fence which separated him from the Harvest People. The Moon-Faced Dog sat on a mound of earth, wagging his tail in a continuous circle.

The Harvest People handed the Old Man a basket and they stood above him on ladders, dropping fruit into the basket. They said, when we are done, we will be finished. And finished is what we want to be most of all.

Tomorrow, the Old Man said. Will you be finished tomorrow also?

Oh, no, the Harvest People said, tomorrow we will be starting. But today we must be finished in order to start again tomorrow. That is the whole idea. If you do not start you never will be finished. And if you are finished, you can only look forward to starting. Once started, finishing is all that is important. You are constantly in a rush from start to finish and from finish to start.

What is the difference then? the Old Man asked but the Harvest People were well into finishing.

They began to drop the apples into the basket so fast that the Old Man had to run in a circle to catch them. The Old Man said, what does the apple see as it falls?

The Harvest People laughed: the apple has no eyes.

Everything has eyes, the Old Man said, because everything has life. Even this apple has life given to it by the tree. Does it end simply because it is picked?

It is going to go into our stomachs, the Harvest People said. If the apple lived there, it would make us sick.

The apple's life is your life for the time being, the Old Man said. It must rot as well as ripen, for it is in rotting that it blooms again. Without the rot of the apple, you would die. Eat it and see how much it nourishes your body. It nourishes your mind. Between the tree and the basket, the apple takes a journey. It is perhaps this journey which supplies the true nourishment.

The apple is ripe when it leaves the tree, the Harvest People said. The apple cannot be rotten or no one will buy it. That is the whole purpose of an apple. To be bought and eaten.

Have you asked the apple if it wishes to be eaten? the Old Man asked. Perhaps it would rather remain on the tree and die in its own way.

The Harvest People laughed. The apple was meant to be picked. What else is an apple for?

Who knows? The Old Man said.

The Harvest People threw all of the rotten apples at the Old Man then. Stop bothering us, they said. We must be finished or else. We must be finished in order to be done. We must be finished or we cannot start again. You have interrupted our whole scheme of things.

The Old Man climbed under the fence and found the Moon-Faced Dog waiting for him. The story that you told was the wrong story, he said reproachfully. His tail had stopped wagging altogether.

What is the right story? asked the Old Man irritably. He was feeling tired and wished to go home and lie down.

The Moon-Faced Dog only walked along in the dust which had begun to rise.

You are no help, the Old Man said. Why do you follow me?

To see that you do not get lost, replied the Moon-Faced Dog. He walked beside the Old Man, casting his shadow to the east, the Place Where Shadows Die in the Path of the Rising Sun. He was going west, toward Revelation, leading the Old Man on.

But the Old Man took no notice of direction. He went along with his head down, dragging the Thread behind him. He tried to let it go once and felt something take its place in his hand. Looking down, he saw that it was the hand of a child. He heard the child asking to be held with an open hand. He saw that the Thread had begun to rise and spread itself before him, bathed in a strange green light.

All the Old Man had to do was follow it, holding the hand of the child who walked in the shade and was not seen for shade is the dwelling place of spirits. The spirit of the child was in the shade and the Old Man was in the shade also. The Old Man was much aware of the child as he went steadily west, spinning out from the Circle of his life. But he did not know how to hold the child with an open hand.

At last the Old Man recognized that they had come a long way, into a land that was unfamiliar.

What are we doing here? the Old Man said, not knowing the place where he found himself. Why do we keep on?

What else is there to do? replied the Moon-Faced Dog.

We could turn around, the Old Man said.

We would not be where we thought we were, said the Moon-Faced Dog. That is the trouble with turning around. You are always in a different place.

Why is it so? the Old Man asked, looking back at the familiar path. Ahead was a path he did not know and he did not want to go there.

Time changes the path continuously, said the Moon-Faced Dog. Time bends it and covers it with dust and misconceptions. So nothing is ever the way you remember it. Even when you think it is exactly the same, it is completely different.

I remember everything, the Old Man said. I remember that the place I left was comfortable. But this place is not comfortable and the place we are approaching will be more uncomfortable yet. He looked ahead and saw nothing there that encouraged him.

The trouble with you is, you see with your memory, said the Moon-Faced Dog. It is a bad habit. That way, you are shaping the path ahead before you even get there. You are not open to anything new.

The Old Man did not like the way the Moon-Faced Dog was speaking to him. I have the right to my thoughts, he said, forming them into a picture of the place he had come from.

It depends if they are lasting thoughts or not, said the Moon-Faced Dog. If they are lasting thoughts, you have a right to them. If they are not lasting thoughts, you must leave them along the path.

Looking back, the Old Man saw that he had dropped some of last year's thoughts behind. He saw that they were not nourished nor welcomed where they fell. He saw last year's thoughts rise and blow away. Ahead of him he saw that next year's thoughts waited for someone to speak them. He opened his mouth and issued Silence. He was not able to speak of what was yet to come.

The Old Man looked at the Moon-Faced Dog who was progressing steadily toward the place he meant to go. What lasting thoughts do you possess? the Old Man asked.

I? said the Moon-faced Dog with an air of superiority. I have no need of thoughts. For me it is enough to be what I am, neither greater nor smaller than what I was meant to be.

Do you wish to see what the world contains? the Old Man asked, pulling down the Thread to form a way for the Moon-Faced Dog to get there.

The world is what I see before me, said the Moon-Faced Dog, stopping to sniff a bush. The world I see before me is neither good nor bad. Everywhere looks the same to me.

Not true, said the Old Man indignantly. Look at this land before us. See how dry and brittle it is. The land we left was green and beautiful. This land is flat. The land we left was full of mountains.

The Moon-Faced Dog scarcely looked around to where the Old Man was pointing. I see no difference to it, he said. Desert and mountains are all the same to me. Today is the same as tomorrow. Night is the same as day.

The Old Man saw it was useless to argue with the Moon-Faced Dog. What is your purpose then? the Old Man asked crossly.

When you find out the secret of that, you will no longer need me, said the Moon-Faced Dog who had begun to smile a little.

But when the Old Man stopped to scratch him behind the ears, he moved away. You may not touch me, said the Moon-Faced Dog. But I can always touch you. I can come into you and out again and you will not be the same. As for you, I have no need for your company.

Leave me then, the Old Man said but even as he spoke the words he knew that the Moon-Faced Dog was necessary to him. He knew that the Moon-Faced Dog would not leave him until the time had come. He went along the path the Moon-Faced Dog had chosen, no longer considering whether it was the right path nor whether the Moon-Faced Dog was leading him into danger. He had begun to hold the child with an open hand.

THE TWO WORLDS
OF BEING

The Old Man and the Moon-Faced Dog continued their journey together which was always to the west, the Direction of Growing, and yet they never seemed to come any closer than they had the day before. When they stopped for the night the Old Man would always ask, how much farther is it?

And the Moon-Faced Dog would always reply, no farther.

But the Old Man could see it was a ridiculous answer since they were not there yet. Then he would always ask, when will we get there?

And the Moon-Faced Dog would always reply, when you get there you will know.

How will I know? the Old Man would always ask.

And the Moon-Faced Dog would always reply, the way you always know.

The Old Man would get angry at the Moon-Faced Dog then and try to beat him with a stick but the dog always went into his shadow where the Old Man could not find him. He would stay there until the Old Man calmed down.

When the Old Man was trying to calm down, he would always ask, do you want to hear a story?

And the Moon-Faced Dog would always reply, it makes no difference to me.

The Old Man would say, I will tell it to you anyhow.

No matter what story he told, the Moon-Faced Dog would always say, the story you told was the wrong story. The Old Man would tell him another one. Sooner or later he believed he would tell the right story.

One day when they had come many miles across the desert in the heat, saying little, the Old Man stopped and had the same conversation with the Moon-Faced Dog that he always had and was going to tell him the same kind of story he always did, then changed his mind.

Today I am going to tell you a new story, the Old Man said.

I care nothing at all about new stories, said the Moon-Faced Dog and pretended to go to sleep. But the Old Man went on with it.

✳ A long time ago I saw that there were Two Worlds of Being. There was the First World that I lived in and the Second World that I dreamed in. I stood between these Two Worlds, thinking I was perfectly balanced. But one day I fell down between them and became lost in the uncertainty which separates the two. I fell down because neither world was strong enough in me.

✗ This is the way it was.

✗ The First World of Being is the easiest place to be because it is the popular world. It is the world where everyone lives, speaking the same language and wearing the same expression. In the First World of Being there is work for the sake of a job and a job for the sake of filling up the time.

There is habit which falls into a hole open at either end. There are excuses which are offered as reason and escape which is offered as solution.

The First World of Being is where everyone is content to live on one floor, going neither up nor down. You cannot ask them why they are there. Even if they knew, they would not believe there was another possibility.

The First World is made of parallel lines and colors already picked out; it is made of identical moods. The First World is a world of slots and keyholes. It is a world into which everything fits that is made and nothing fits that is not made.

The First World is a world of repetition for the sake of sounding alike. It is a world of sitting down for the sake of not moving your feet. It is a world of standing still even when you are moving on.

The First World has power but no strength. It has comfort but no concern. It has eyes but no vision. It has ears but does not hear. It has a tongue but utters only noise. In the First World you can spend your entire life with people and yet not know one true friend. In this world, friends are counted for wearing the same face; they are counted for agreeing to carry sameness from one generation to the next.

In this world the waters are shallow and you will not even get wet. The rocks have been taken away so you will not have to go around. The earth has been tamed so you will have nothing to explore. The sky has been accounted for so there is no mystery there. In the First World there is an explanation for everything and a calculation to solve questions that should not be asked.

The First World is papered with mirrors and the sounds are all of echoes. The roads are paved with destinations but

no one ever gets there. No one chooses an uphill path or a
road that is not on the map. The First World is built to
specification. It follows a ready-made plan consisting of du-
plicate keys and windows which do not open and doors which
lock from both sides. The First World rises on elevators and
falls on its limitations.

The First World expands but does not grow. It burns
but offers no warmth. It has learned to conquer the dark but
still there is no light. It buries itself in riches but still it has
not overcome its poverty.

The First World is where you have been long before you
get there. It is a world you can never leave unless you leave
yourself behind. This world seems right because everyone is
there. It seems indisputable for there is no one to argue with.
This world is a locked world where people imprison themselves.

The First World is a world of judgment but no justice.
It is a world of balance but no equality. It is a world where
everything costs something and what is free costs more.

The Moon-Faced Dog stopped wagging his tail in a continuous circle. What a curious story, he said. Go on with it.

The Old Man said, the First World of Being is always
jealous of the Second and does everything to destroy it for
the two are opposite and incompatible, just as day and night.
If you have discovered peace, the First World will offer position for it. If you have accepted wonder, the First World will
kill it with work. This world looks favorably on those who go
to school but are not educated and those who recite and are
convinced by reciting. The First World is impressed by facts
to prove its fiction.

When I was a Young Boy I put on my First World face
and went to live in a city to see if it was a good place. I saw

how easy it is to be comfortable there. The First World is one of competition and reward. It is one of appearance and attitude. It is one which offers money for the ambition you possess. It offers recognition for the only life you own. But the First World will not answer if you cry to it nor will it give you comfort in the night. It will not give consolation but offers conditions which always look alike. The First World requires considerable aim for the target is undefined.

The Moon-Faced Dog appeared not to be listening for he was looking the other way. I have not heard of such a world, he said. It means nothing at all to me.

He started to walk away but the Old Man stopped him. Then perhaps you will recognize the Second World, he said. Nature is the whole idea of this world.

I know nothing of nature, said the Moon-Faced Dog. I am what I am. I do not know which world is which.

✳ The First World is the outer world, the Old Man said. It is a permanent address. But the Second World is the inner world. It is without location and yet it is at home everywhere. The Second World is without season, for all seasons are present at the same time. It is without knowledge, for all is known to it. It is without ambition, for nothing surpasses itself. It is without conflict, for there are no odds to it.

The Second World is where you must go and keep a vigil over the earth. It is where you must spend your inheritance. It is where you must share the little bit you have learned with a brother who has learned no more. Even then, knowledge will not solve its mystery. The Second World is as it should be, a never-ending mystery.

The Second World is where the dead take root in the sky and the living are uprooted from themselves. It is where you must go dressed in rain, wearing only its gentleness. It is where you must introduce yourself and yet not give your name. It is where you must walk in reverence, for all is religion there.

To enter the Second World you must escape the prison of your body and become one with the universe. You must get used to inconvenience and the disturbance of cold. You must learn to wait for that Time of Illumination and the appearance of a Positive Force. You may see it as the eternity of a single afternoon. You may see it in the face of a child. You may see it in Smoke and Rain. You may see it in your mind alone.

But do not think you will remember such a vision. You will take away only an imprint like a leaf pressed against the earth or a stone taken up from where it was. It will have a certain outline but where is the leaf? Where is the stone? Gone, just as the vision is gone.

So you must seek it again and again. You must seek it in various ways and positions and attitudes. You must seek it away from people. You must experience this vision with your mouth and with your hands and feet. You must experience it with your eyes closed for you cannot see with your eyes alone. You must experience it with pain which bears the comfort of truth. You must experience it with grief which opens a door to the deepest sort of life. You must experience it with joy which rises above all petty distraction.

I am confused, said the Moon-Faced Dog who had a life of his own. What is grief? What is joy? Be more specific in what you say.

Very well, the Old Man said and tried to think of a way to explain things to the Moon-Faced Dog.

Every part of nature is in the Second World, the Old Man said. It lives and dies according to the nature it has. The

Second World requires learning how to see what is truly important about this nature.

You can spend a day watching a spider spin its web and that is a Second World thing.

You can watch a butterfly and a bee coming to the same thistle to die and that is a Second World thing.

You can see how much work it is for an ant to carry home a fly and that is a Second World thing.

You can watch an eagle soaring across the sky or a robin pulling a worm out of the ground and those are Second World things.

You can listen to the wind in the trees or hear the music of a stream and those are Second World things.

You can watch the sky at night and realize how small you are and that is a Second World thing.

I have seen all that, said the Moon-Faced Dog with a yawn. Where I come from, Second World things are not important at all.

The Old Man wondered how to make the Moon-Faced Dog understand.

The Second World is the true center of life, the Old Man said. It is where anything can happen for all things are possible there. It is a world of perhaps and why not. It is where there is peace and quiet and where the spirit finds rest. One Way is always there and One Hand is always there. In the Second World of Being there is a strong fortress made entirely of belief. There is a flowing river which carries only hope. In this world you find out why you must go on even when it is easier letting go. You find out if you are up to the task of life.

The Second World is other things as well, the Old Man

said, noticing that the Moon-Faced Dog was sniffing the wind
and not listening to him.

The Second World is a world of untying the knot. It is
the world of finding One Way. It is a world of hearing a new
voice in old stones and a whisper in newborn leaves. It is the
reason for flowers and the reason for wings.

The Second World is the world of having no name. It is
a world of no address. It is where you go alone and do not
know loneliness. It is where you die and do not know death.
It is where you are taught and still know nothing. It is where
there are no answers even though new questions are always
asked.

Come, the Old Man said, we will journey into the Second World together simply by being alone. Close your eyes
and tell me what you see there.

But the Moon-Faced Dog only sat wagging his tail in a
continuous circle. He was of a certain nature and had no use
for either world.

The Old Man was eager to finish his story.

The Two Worlds are always present, the Old Man said.
You must belong to one world or the other. You cannot belong to both.

When I was young I was impressed with what the First
World had to offer. I desired to be rich and powerful. But I
desired peacefulness also. I had to make a living in the First
World in those days. But I desired the quiet heart as well. As
it was, the Two Worlds were not possible at the same time. I
ran around and around, trying to connect them together.

What happened to me was this.

I lay between the Two Worlds of Being wondering what
to do. Then one day out of the First World came a Blue Locust who stood in the middle of a green field. He said to me,

climb on my back and I will take you on a journey through my field. It is a safe journey and at the end of it is a wonderful house which has in it everything you need.

I asked the Blue Locust what I had to do for it and he replied, you cannot take the Second World with you. You will have to leave it behind forever. Where you are going, you will not need it.

I asked him why this was so but he refused to tell me. He only said to me, everyone else is going there so it must be the right place after all.

But I did not believe him.

Then all at once a huge Red Butterfly with wings made of sunlight appeared above my head, blocking out my view. He said to me, climb on my back and the wind will take us wherever it chooses to go. It is neither up nor down, forward nor backward. There are demons where we are going and they can devour you. There is also a place of rest but I do not know how to get there. It is up to you to find the signs of the route we are to take.

I asked the Red Butterfly why I should go with him since it seemed an uncertain place. And he replied, there is no reason. There is only curiosity.

I became furious with the Red Butterfly then and went after him, intending to kill him. The Blue Locust stood by me, offering to help. He said, when all the Red Butterflies are dead, we will have no more trouble. The world will be the property of the Blue Locusts. I will help you to destroy the world of the Red Butterfly.

I asked him what world this was but he was in his own world which was the green field, ripe and ready to be stripped.

The Red Butterfly rose with the wind and I, having no

wings at the time, rose with the music which played in the dark. The wind was always ahead of the music and the Butterfly, being lighter, was always ahead of me. Sometimes when he slept I crept up on him and would have killed him except that I had begun to notice his beauty. But the Butterfly was my enemy and so I pursued him all through the summer that we were going through. I pursued him as long as the music lasted.

When the music stopped, I was in the middle of a great hot desert. There was no water to drink. There were lizards with enormous teeth which came out over their mouths. There were gigantic birds with claws as long as my body. I was terrified to be in that place and I wished that I had gone with the Blue Locust instead. I began to walk across the desert, searching for water. All that I had to protect me was a desire to get to the other side.

The more I walked, the easier it became. The desert had plants in it which were very beautiful. I stopped to drink from them. I stopped to talk to every living thing I came across. I saw many things I had never seen before. Pretty soon I was not concerned about how long it took to get to the other side. I walked along, taking whatever time it took because the desert was important to me. It had so much life in it. Wherever I looked, I saw a new thing. I was not thirsty for I was able to find water in the smallest places.

At the end of the desert, I kept on going. I could not stop. There was a deep forest which began along a river and rose to the top of a mountain. Looking at it, I knew I had to see what the river and the forest and the mountain contained. The way a leaf unfolded in the sun was a mystery which I had no wish to solve. For me, it was enough to observe things happening. And so it was with everything I found there.

When I got to the top of the mountain, the Red Butterfly was waiting for me. He said, climb on my back and I will take you home. Winter is coming on and soon I must be going. Do you wish to ride with me or not?

I had no desire to kill the Red Butterfly anymore. I had no desire to climb on his back either. I said to him, I will wait for winter with you.

But then on the wind I heard all the voices of the First World calling to me, offering me all the rewards it had. I saw everything float up and surround me with angry faces. The Blue Locust came too and rebuked me for taking so much time. He said, it is almost too late to come to my world.

I asked him what world it was and he said, the popular world which is the safest world of all.

I knew then that the world of the Blue Locust was the First World of Being. I did not even bother to thank him since he had given me nothing at all.

I closed my eyes and lay down on the Butterfly's back. I said to him, fly away with me. We will go with the wind wherever it chooses to go.

But the Red Butterfly said, it is too late. Autumn has already come. I can no longer fly. You will have to wait until spring when everything is born again.

The Red Butterfly collapsed and died. When his body went back into the earth, many things were revealed to me. I knew that the world of the Red Butterfly was the Second World of Being. I gave thanks to the Red Butterfly for showing it to me.

But then the Blue Locust descended on me. He was very angry and he said, you have no business here. You belong in my fields with everyone else. He opened his mouth and picked me up and started down the mountain to take me back to the First World. I struck at him with all my strength but he was very powerful. He laughed at me and said, it is no use. The Red Butterfly has died and his world has died with him.

But I knew that the Blue Locust did not speak the truth because where the Red Butterfly died, a new plant had already started to grow. And as it grew, a certain song came from it and went with me and I knew that it would be in my ears forever. The song was the song of everything I had seen.

I said to the Blue Locust, it is no longer a question of choosing the First World or the Second. The Second World has chosen me. It will travel with me always no matter where I go.

The Blue Locust stopped where he was and set me down. He said, you are not easily deceived. You have discovered which world is which.

Because winter was coming on, the Blue Locust prepared to die also.

I went back to the First World and existed in it but the Second World was where I truly lived.

The Second World became the home within my body. The Second World was where everything of value took place.

There were tears in the Old Man's eyes and he brushed them aside. The Thread was resting gently on his shoulders, saturated with the thoughts he had just put into it. It was a good story that the Old Man had told and yet the Moon-Faced Dog sat impassively in the dust, wagging his tail in a continuous circle, gazing out across the dry land where the river had cut a deep and winding path.

Did you hear my story? the Old Man asked.

Of course, said the Moon-Faced Dog, getting up to relieve himself.

Did you like it? the Old Man asked, fearful that his words had been for nothing.

The Moon-Faced Dog lifted his leg on a rock and turned his head to the sky to see what was happening there.

I have heard it before, he said. He turned his back on the Old Man and began to consider the place in which he found himself.

Was it the right story? the Old Man asked but the Moon-Faced Dog only ignored him; he was watching the direction of the water.

Was it the wrong story then? the Old Man asked.

He was beginning to believe the Moon-Faced Dog was out to trick him. He was beginning to wonder why he had come so far with the Moon-Faced Dog. He was beginning to wish he was far away from that place which was unfamiliar to him.

But the eyes of the Moon-Faced Dog drew him down to the river. He looked up and saw that the land above him rose like the wings of a bird, dark and folding out from the slim point he found himself in. Between the two wings he saw the blue of the sky and the Mountain blending into it so he could not tell which was which. He could not tell if he was up or down or which was the first dimension; he could not decide if he had been to this spot before or if it was yet to come. He could only perceive that the stream divided the Mountain and formed two wings on either side of himself; he could only perceive that he was unable to get out.

I am lost, the Old Man cried but the Moon-Faced Dog only laughed.

Come down and help me, the Old Man begged but the Moon-Faced Dog only laughed some more.

Help yourself, he said and began to move away.

The Old Man struggled to go up, against the energy of water. He watched the water flowing and he spoke to it in a silent voice and his silent words were thus carried on down the river and out to the sea. Looking up toward the Mountain where the river began, the Old Man saw the slim silvery thread of water working its way to him. This water contained the thoughts that were yet to come while the water below him contained the thoughts he already had. The Old Man sat where he was, between his past and future thoughts.

THE FIVE LESSONS

The Old Man left the Circle of his life and found a Stillpoint which is the way the life Circle becomes a spiral, moving ever outward as it progresses on a circular route that is unbroken. The Stillpoint was suspension of time and it was also the Old Man suspended above time; it was a now which has no limitation. The Old Man perceived the Stillpoint as peace and was much strengthened; he perceived it as regeneration and rest. The Stillpoint was where the Circle slowed down but did not stop; it was where the Old Man perceived certain changes within the Circle itself. It was where the Old Man began to say the things inside him that needed saying for the sake of being where he was.

The Old Man said, I have gone deep into the earth and out again. I have gone to the World of the Sky and come back. The going was always experience while the coming back was Essence which is a way of seeing and believing. It is a way of throwing out what is not important and a way of guarding what is most important of all. Essence is ultimate thought and ultimate action; it is the ultimate reason. It is this Essence which lies upon the Thread. Essence is what life is made of and it is a life larger than the one I live. All things matter for nothing is without life. Nothing is without Essence.

This is the way life should be in our minds.

It was the first lesson that the Old Man taught and the Wind heard it and took his words and blew them to the south on the wings of the Dove who carried Understanding which is the first power.

The Old Man said, I am at home with myself. I am comfortable with the body which surrounds me. I know the limitations of it. I do not ask it for more. My body is the house I live in. I am protected by it just as it is protected by me. I have come to understand that it is a temporary house. I have lived and will go on living in many houses which are made of skin or wood or rock or air. These houses are strong but not so strong that you cannot kill them. The houses have to be cared for so they will last a long time and provide a place for Essence to reside.

I recognize the spirit which lives in my house. It is no longer a stranger to me. I have seen it before in different places. Only now has it come into my house to stay for all time. It brought light to shine in the dark corners of my house. It brought fire which I can turn to when the world becomes too cold. It brought nourishment too. When I eat the spirit, my hunger becomes satisfied. You cannot tempt me with other food. I am so full that there is no room for anything more.

I have put my house in order from the inside out. I can go anywhere with this house and nothing will bother it. The winds can only shake it but not tear it down. The rains cannot come in because I have sealed up all the cracks. For now, my house is the best one I can make. What will destroy my house is time. Even then, the inside will live on.

A man who is at home in his skin is at home in the universe.

It was the second lesson the Old Man had taught and the Water heard it and took his words and flowed with them to the east on the fins of the Spotted Fish who carried Awareness which is the second power.

The Old Man said, I will never come to the end of seeing or believing because I will never come to the end of being. My blood whispers to me all of the time. It is blood made of eggshells and mud and bone. My feet, which have taken me everywhere, are the feet of the first fish who came out of the water and stood on dry land. My arms are the arms of the first creature who reached up to pick food from the trees. My eyes are the eyes of the eagle. My ears are the ears of the deer. My nose is the nose of the coyote. Everything that is part of me was part of something else. I am connected to all things and all things are connected to me. I am the first breath and the last. I am everything in between.

The Old Man, being in the Stillpoint of time, was able to see himself as he had been and would yet become. He was able to see that he always waited with his head up; he was able to see himself becoming greater because of the hope he placed in waiting. He was able to see that he had already been greater than all he would ever be and that all he could ever be was still not great enough. He was able to see that there was only one choice left and that was not to run away from the Circle of his life.

I am one footstep going on, the Old Man said.

It was the third lesson the Old Man had taught and the Fire heard it and took his words and burned with them to the west on the tongue of the Buffalo who carried Faith which is the third power.

The Old Man said, each time I have gone inside myself I have recognized the spirit that dwells there. I have recognized it in the Shadows and I saw what was to come. I have recognized it in the Illumination of the day and I saw that there is no death, only a change of worlds. I recognized it in the Rock and I saw why I have been singled out. I have learned about my roots which took me into the deepest part of myself.

But I refuse to tell what's at the center of it. It is up to you to find out.

It was the fourth lesson the Old Man had taught and the Earth heard it and took his words and buried them in the north on the claws of the Bear who carried Introspection which is the fourth power.

When his lessons were finished, the Old Man let out his breath and gave up something of himself.

The Four Things That Are Heard said in one voice:

This is the moment that is the Essence of all moments to come and all moments that are past. This is the moment of Now which grows and dies in the same moment. This is the moment which comes but once in a lifetime and is the lifetime we have spoken of. This is the moment of gain and the moment of loss. This is the moment to be and to go on being.

The Thread hovered above the Old Man, then rose and encircled the Four Things That Are Heard. The Thread went higher and higher, taking the Essence of the Old Man with it.

The Four Things That Are Heard said:

The Thread will not come back to the earth unless the Old Man brings it.

The Thread will vanish forever unless the Old Man understands it.

The Thread will turn the sun blue and the moon red unless the Old Man believes it.

The Thread will break unless the Old Man carries it.

If he does all these things, the Thread will live on but the Old Man will die because of it. The Old Man will die because he is the Bearer of the Thread and nothing more. When the Thread is passed, the Old Man's purpose will be fulfilled.

The prophecy of the Four Things That Are Heard was a prophecy that had come true many times over, ever since mankind found something to believe in which was not the common belief. The prophecy's fulfillment was the reward of having belief at all.

With that the Four Things That Are Heard broke loose from the Thread and fell to the earth as Rock and Wind and Water and Fire. The Old Man found himself alone with the Thread which began to wind itself around him, tighter and tighter so that he saw and heard nothing. There was only blackness and silence and the Old Man was in the place below the Second World of Being which is the Place of Transmutation. In that place the Old Man perceived that there was yet another lesson for him to learn but he did not know what it was. The Old Man held his breath and felt his Being change for the final lesson.

The Moon-Faced Dog had stopped wagging his tail and was looking down at the river where he had left the Old Man. All that he saw now was a tiny Black Ant crawling across the face of the rock, not knowing which way to go for he changed his direction often. The Moon-Faced Dog noticed the trouble the Black Ant was having and said to it, climb on my tail and I will take you where you want to go.

I do not know where I want to go, cried the Black Ant. I am trying to learn direction.

Then it will not make any difference, said the Moon-Faced Dog. Climb on and I will see that you get there.

Thank you, said the Black Ant. But I am afraid I will not get anywhere with you.

The Moon-Faced Dog placed one huge paw beside him and the Black Ant almost fell into a crack in the rock which was deep and dark.

See what you have made me do, said the Black Ant, resuming his path on the rock.

I will help you, said the Moon-Faced Dog, standing in the direction the Black Ant was trying to take. Just take hold of my tail.

And he began to wag it in a continuous circle.

Move out of the way, said the Black Ant. I have no time to lose. He spoke as bravely as he could but he was terrified of the Moon-Faced Dog who was ten thousand times bigger.

The Moon-Faced Dog lay down then, covering the entire rock. You will have to climb over me, he said. Or else you will have to go the long way around.

The Black Ant looked and saw that the rock was so big it would take him too long to go the long way around. He started to climb on the tail of the Moon-Faced Dog, then said, how do I know you will not kill me?

Because I have given you my word, said the Moon-Faced Dog. It is not my nature to destroy.

But the Black Ant did not believe him.

The Birds from the Four Directions appeared then, forming a circle around the Black Ant.

The bird from the east was the Magpie and she said, I will take you in my direction. Climb in my mouth.

Oh no, said the Black Ant, for he knew the Magpie would take him to the Coyote.

The bird from the west was the Spotted Eagle and he said, I will take you in my direction. Climb in my mouth.

Oh no, said the Black Ant, for he knew the Spotted Eagle would drop him from the sky.

The bird from the north was the Hawk and he said, I will take you in my direction. Climb in my mouth.

Oh no, said the Black Ant, for he knew the Hawk would eat him.

The bird from the south was the Redheaded Woodpecker and she said, I will take you in my direction. Climb in my mouth.

Oh no, said the Black Ant, for he knew that the Redheaded Woodpecker would feed him to her young.

Very well, said the birds, stay where you are.

The flapping of their wings nearly blew the Black Ant off the rock and he had to hold on to a hair on the tail of the Moon-Faced Dog with all his might. He had to keep from blowing into the crack which was very close to him. It was so deep that he could not see where it went.

Move out of the way, he said to the Moon-Faced Dog, I am in a hurry to be going.

But the Moon-Faced Dog only yawned and said, be quiet or I will lick your face.

The Animals from the Four Directions appeared then and sat in the Four Corners.

The animal from the east was the Coyote and he said, it would be very easy to step on you.

The animal from the west was the Buffalo and he said, it would be very easy to breathe on you.

The animal from the north was the Bear and he said, it would be very easy to shed my tears on you.

The animal from the south was the Deer and he said, it would be very easy to deposit my waste on you.

The Black Ant was so frightened that he tried to hide from the animals by climbing into the ear of the Moon-Faced Dog.

I am afraid, he cried.

And the Moon-Faced Dog said, fear will not save you.

The animals laughed together and said, come out. We are all tame. We will not hurt you.

The Black Ant did not know whether to believe them or not but he came out of the Dog's ear anyway for he was of a curious nature. All he could see was the shape of the animals which filled up the entire sky. The animals came closer to him so they formed a complete Circle.

Spare my life, cried the Black Ant, falling into their shadow. He tried not to be seen but felt the power of their eyes upon him. He pulled one hair out of the tail of the Moon-Faced Dog and held it to him.

Out of the crack in the rock there suddenly came a swarm of Red Ants who were all relatives of the Black Ant. What is the matter with you? they said. All you have to do is slip into that crack beside you. You can escape from everything. Not even the biggest animal can find you.

The Black Ant replied, I did not think of it. I was too busy going one way.

You are the smallest of creatures, the Red Ants said.

You can only see life from the lowest level. Your face is always to the ground. Your horizon is no more than a stone. Yet you think you are greater than the animals and the birds. There is no humility to you.

A snowflake could break your back.

A grain of sand could suffocate you.

A drop of rain could drown you.

A particle of dust could carry you away.

The crack is all that counts, the Red Ants said. The crack is the only thing between you and death. Hurry and jump into it.

I do not have the courage, the Black Ant said.

It will not save you anyway, said the Moon-Faced Dog.

What will save me? cried the Black Ant who was poised at the edge of the crack. The Red Ants came running, intending to push him in but the Black Ant closed his eyes and jumped, taking the hair which belonged to the Moon-Faced Dog. The hair kept him from falling too fast; it was something for him to hang on to.

What ally goes with you? he heard the Moon-Faced Dog shout as he fell deeper and deeper into the crack not knowing where he would land.

Trust, the Black Ant shouted back for he had come to a place where trust and darkness meet. He did not hurt himself for the hair was a cushion which broke his fall.

When he came out of the crack, the Old Man said, we are put here to help one another. We are put here to try. That is all we can do.

We are not separate from one another. We are part of a universal fire.

It was the fifth lesson that the Old Man taught and the Moon-Faced Dog heard his words and began to wag his tail in a continuous circle, taking Trust with him so that it went in all directions.

The Old Man began to move away from the Stillpoint into that part of his Circle of life which was still expanding.

THE SEED POINT
AND THE ROOT POCKET

The Old Man slept until he was rested and his body was in tune with itself. He slept until his vision was without clouds and the song he sang was of starlight and sun and wind and rain. His song was the music he danced to, harder and harder, until at last his feet wore a hole in the earth and his head went through the roof of the sky.

The Old Man awoke refreshed. He looked back along the Thread he was carrying and saw his song taken apart and made into single notes which went in different directions. He saw that the notes always kept rising until someone pulled them down from the sky. He saw that the notes were waiting everywhere for someone to hear them. He saw too the silence between the notes. The silence was the people standing still. The silence was what they lived in. The echo of silence was fear.

Then the Old Man saw that certain notes pulled away from the Thread and went down and became whole songs of infinite verse. The people living in the songs moved with them. The songs were their inner rhythms and so they were always dancing to them. The songs were the breath of the People of the Sun House Moon.

The Old Man got up and made his Morning Circle on the ground the way he always did. He pressed himself into it and said, lie down and feel the Earth Mother stirring from her sleep. Encircle her with your body and feel her heart beating in a rhythm that is the earth's song. Within this Circle, all life is working in one way or another. The leaves that lie on the surface, the spider who waits for the fly, the worm who is turning the soil, the stream that flows nearby, the tree that is growing from a seed, all this is an Earth Circle. Beneath this is another and so on down through every layer of life that has ever been here. From this Circle you can feel what is still happening deep within; you can feel into the center of the earth and out again for the Earth Circle expands like a beam of light shining in the dark.

But on the other side of the Earth Circle is the Sky Circle, the Old Man said and turned over, looking up at the trees which stood over him and the rock on either side and beyond that the first light starting to appear in the east and the last of the stars going home.

In the Sky Circle there are the sun and moon and stars. There are clouds and rain and snow. There is wind which is cold and wind which is warm. There is wind from a certain direction. In the Sky Circle are all of the winged creatures who are the only creatures able to separate themselves from the Earth Circle any time they choose. The winged creatures are offering the benefit of freedom. They are offering a world without limitation. If you want to leave this earth for a time, then align yourself with a winged creature and go up and see how small the earth really is. Then you will be able to laugh at what is happening to you here.

The Sky Circle is endless. Out there somewhere the Sky Circle meets the Earth Circle and what is formed is called a True Circle. It is the Seed Point and the Root Pocket. It is the Womb of Seasons, the Eternal Pause and Question.

The Old Man prayed to the Earth Circle and the Sky Circle and everything within. The Old Man gave thanks and said, to make a Circle is to make an attitude toward the day. To make a Circle is to release a Positive Force. To make a Circle is to receive the Light of the Great Spirit.

The Old Man was purified and he had grown and expanded to a certain state which was to become identified for it was a Day of Identification. It was a Day of Committing Oneself to Being.

The Old Man stretched his arms toward the sky. The Moon-Faced Dog, being within a Circle already, did not bother to make one but began to eat what he had found.

The Old Man said, how beautiful the sky is. The sun is painting it gold with light to make a proper path for its arrival. What a priceless gold it is and the red is the robe of the universe. Every beautiful moment is captured in a now that is opening out in all directions.

The Moon-Faced Dog continued to eat and did not look up.

Here is your explanation for life, the Old Man said, but you can only grasp it for a moment. Then you must be moving onward with the sun into another day and a new experience. Tomorrow you will have to start all over again for tomorrow's explanation is yesterday's question and today's question is not even formed. When it is, tomorrow's explanation will not be the right explanation, for the question is no longer there. It has taken a new direction and become its own answer but it is not an answer you will recognize. It is an answer you will forget even before you remember. The answer is always there and never there. The answer is always trying to discover an opening in your mind through which the spirit may pass.

The Old Man sat down, having made his Circle and finished his prayer and waited for the sun, speaking to the Moon-Faced Dog in order to hear the words aloud.

The growing and dying of the day brings a new question which turns and twists in your mind all through the night, the Old Man said. And there in the dawn is your answer but it disappears because a new question is always forming. It may be the same old question over and over. I do not know if it is. I only know that the dawn makes each question seem new to me and my answers very old and insignificant. I only know I must keep following the sun and die a little death each day with it. In that way I am purified. I can make a new beginning which is no beginning at all but the continuation of One Idea.

What Idea? asked the Moon-Faced Dog who used to find them in gatherings of men dissatisfied and men demented and men dreaming of new paths to take. Nowadays the Ideas he found were all to one disadvantage or another. Nowadays he found a similarity to them.

Listen, the Old Man said, and I will tell you a story about the way in which One Idea came into being. I will tell you about the creation of the world.

I am listening, said the Moon-Faced Dog but he was bored by it all, having been witness to good Ideas and bad and seeing they were all the same. He was trying to avoid Ideas as best he could.

This is how I remember it, the Old Man said and drew himself up in the position of a storyteller, wrapping his red blanket around him and extending his arm so the Moon-Faced Dog was obliged to follow it, seeing that it pointed to a Rock which was written on.

This is what the Rock said as the Old Man revealed the words he found upon it.

A long time ago the earth was locked in continuous day and the sun howled and the moon had no expression at all but was red and defiant. The stars were all on fire and dropped out of the sky one by one, caught at the edge of it by the Left-Handed Hunter who put them into his belt. The earth was all Fire at first, raging continuously, with nothing to put it out. There was only air to keep it going.

There was a need for rain and so rain came, cooling off Fire that was earth and making Mist to conceal the earth from the sun which continued to howl. The rain made an ocean and that was all there was, an ocean rolling and tossing and void.

There was a need for land and so land appeared out of the ocean and gave it Rock to hollow out. Land gave ocean a shore for its waves to touch. Land was a way for ocean to have an edge for it is Water which always wins out, even over Rock.

There was a need for birds and so birds came and filled up the sky.

There was a need for animals and so animals came and filled up the earth.

There was a need for flowers and so flowers came. There was a need for grass and so grass came. There was a need for ants and spiders and snakes and toads and caterpillars and vultures and weasles and coyotes and every living thing. They all came when they were needed.

Nothing was made uselessly. Everything that was made

came from the same Maker, each in its own time and position. The land and the oceans and the rivers, the animals, the
birds, the fishes, and the monsters—they came and went and
went and came again in a different form entirely for nothing
truly died. Not the mountain which exploded nor the sea
which dried up nor the fish which grew feet in order to walk
on land.

Hurry up, said the Moon-Faced Dog. I am waiting for
One Idea.

I'm getting to it, the Old Man said. You have no patience at all.

At last everything was in its place and there was a place
for everything and nature was complete in time and place,
having expanded into every corner and every creature so that
all was working as one and nothing was ever made that did
not fit such unity.

The earth was perfect in that time and all things were
perfect in that place. The days and nights and seasons were
all perfect. The fishes and birds and creatures were all perfect.
Everything fit into a plan which included the tiniest insect
and the most insignificant plant which was not insignificant
at all for it served a purpose, perhaps to nourish a particular
ant which in turn was food for a bird. The scheme was so vast
and so complicated and so perfect that one thing could not
be removed from it without the scheme collapsing.

And so it was for the larger part of time which was no
time at all for there was no measurement of it. Ten thousand
winters were as a single moment and a single moment was as
ten thousand winters. It made no difference at all.

There was everything on earth at that time and yet there
was one thing absent and that was the presence of an Idea. In
all of nature, an Idea could not be found, not in the birds

which sang so sweetly nor in the rivers which had one true course down to the sea nor in the trees growing upward into light nor in the animals who always behaved in one particular way.

The animals without Ideas did not make war upon one another nor create cities nor write down their stories nor draw upon the rocks the way life was. What would have been the use of that?

The birds without Ideas did not do anything except fly the way the Maker wanted them to. The fishes without Ideas did not do anything except swim the way the Maker wanted them to. The fish had no power over the birds and the birds had no power over the fish and the animals had no power either, except to nourish themselves. These things did not kill uselessly nor did they destroy for the sake of destruction. They were without Ideas and so they did not think of good or evil. Their purpose was to be the way they were.

A tree was content to be a tree. A snail was content to be a snail. A blackbird was content to be a blackbird. A mouse was content to be a mouse. And so on with every animal and fish and bird and plant and tree. The earth was content being what it was meant to be in a certain time and position.

Who was to say if someday the mouse would not be an eagle in another life or that a great fish of the sea would not be the smallest ant in another life? Nothing worried about it because it was not their nature to worry. Everything on earth accepted what was. They did not try to change the eagle into a fly or make the fly greater than he was meant to be.

Hurry up, said the Moon-Faced Dog who cared nothing at all about the way the world was created. He yawned and pretended to go to sleep. But the Old Man continued anyway.

Everything was perfect on the earth at that time. Everything could have gone on forever the way it was except for the appearance of mankind. Mankind was not needed but came anyway because it was time for him to come. Mankind was put here to decide what he would do with the beautiful garden that was the earth in those days. Mankind was put here to be in harmony or not in harmony with all that was around him.

But mankind was the first thing to be made by the Maker that could decide which way he wanted life to be. The Maker gave some things wings and some things fins and other things four legs and still other things leaves and trunks and roots, but he gave mankind a certain mind that was different. And in this mind the Maker planted One Idea and sat back to see what mankind would do with it.

Now the minute that mankind appeared, the world was no longer perfect. No matter where he went, mankind did not fit into his surroundings. He was always extra. He was always changing whatever he found or destroying whatever he found or trying to make things better by making them worse. Mankind believed that the earth was a present from the Maker but he did not bother to thank him for it. Mankind took this gift and left.

Mankind brought tools and ways of speaking with words. He brought religions and ways of explanation. He brought governments and ways of fighting wars. He brought diseases and hatreds and causes. But he brought appreciation and courage and understanding also. He brought a hope and a dream and a song. He brought ways to live in reverence, but in the end he did not use them very well. In the end mankind destroyed the earth.

I could have told you that, said the Moon-Faced Dog

who had been watching the condition of the earth for a long time now, ever since mankind appeared with One Idea. He could see no advantage to it and so turned himself around so he did not have to look at the Old Man any more. His face was to the sky which was the only thing left he could rely on as long as an airplane was not going by or smoke from the cities did not get in his eyes.

But the Old Man was not listening. He was trying to explain things to the Moon-Faced Dog now that he had gotten his attention at long last.

There is but One Idea, the Old Man said. But there are opposite sides to it just as there are opposites to everything. Mankind must choose which side he wants to be on.

The Moon-Faced Dog did not care about opposite sides to anything. It was his nature to live in one way only without having to make a choice at all. He began to look around then for the path he was to take, but the Old Man continued to explain things, as was his nature to do:

On one side of the Idea there is a certain lake which is endless and deep. You can pull anything you need out of it, even when you believe the lake to be dry. If there is a day when you need courage, you can pull courage out of it. If there is a day when you are in search of hope, you can pull hope out of it. If you need strength when everyone is against you, then you can pull strength out of the lake.

In this lake there is the goodness of strong belief. There is the satisfaction of hard work. There is the love of women and men and children. There is the admiration of friends. There is laughter and song bubbling out of this lake. There is the promise of play. There is a game with a ball. There is an unforgettable song.

In this lake there is discovery of endless sorts. There is

appetite; there is co-operation and investment. There is no guarantee nor expectation in this lake. There is no thanks nor pride. There is only swimming and learning how to breathe in water. There is only growing accustomed to the water itself. The deeper you go, the less important reasons become; swimming is all that is important. Swimming is the only thing to do. When you learn how to swim in this lake, you will have found the secret of One Idea. You will have forgotten the other side.

The Moon-Faced Dog did not care for swimming and so he avoided water. He was sniffing the ground to find out which way his path went.

You are always talking, the Moon-Faced Dog complained. Where I come from, nothing has to speak.

The Old Man looked up. I know nothing about you, he said in surprise, realizing that in all their travels together, the Moon-Faced Dog had not told about himself. Why do you do not speak? the Old Man asked. Why do you not tell a story?

That is my nature, said the Moon-Faced Dog crossly. He was eager to leave but his path had become obscured. He could not make a new path. He could only find the old one in order to make his way to where he was supposed to be going.

I am obliged to speak, the Old Man said. Do me the courtesy of listening.

As you please, said the Moon-Faced Dog and sat down to wait for his path to arise.

On the opposite side of the lake is an empty pit, guarded by five huge stones. If you can push any one of them aside you may gain entrance to the pit. You may fill it with whatever your stone contains.

The first stone is dazzling white like a bright star plunging through the sky. The first stone is Greed and you cannot help but try and push it into the pit. With this stone you can fill the pit with gold. You can learn to disguise Greed as assistance to the unfortunate or as an explanation which appears to be right. If you move the first stone, you will be admired but not respected, envied but not trusted for your opinion, obeyed but not secured in loyalty. This sparkling white stone is not enough by itself. You will not rest until you have moved another stone into the pit.

The second stone that guards the pit is a brilliant green. You can do nothing except try and move it. The second stone is Power and you must have it, no matter what it costs. With this stone you can fill up the pit with governments and armies and companies and cities which bear your name. The green stone is what you must possess to empty out the minds of men. It is what you must possess to cut their lives in half for this stone is very sharp. But it will not cut the spirit in two. Long after you have conquered what you set out to control, the spirit will be around somewhere and you will go crazy trying to capture it. You will sell the Power of the second stone in order to find out how to do it. Even then, you will not be able to.

What a beautiful stone there is sitting in the middle—the third stone is a blinding, brilliant red. All of the fires of the earth are in it and the energy of the sun bursts within it but look, the third stone is rolling backward. Do not waste a minute but go after it and shove it in the pit. This third stone is Ignorance. With this stone you can fill the pit with broken hearts and minds which have given up. This red stone will become your ticket to murder and theft and invasion. The third stone is the most useful stone of all. You can go the way of it believing you have arrived at a point where your Ignorance does not matter.

But now you see the fourth stone guarding the pit, so blue and cold like ice which goes well with the fire of the third stone. The blue stone is also rolling backward and there is a temptation to let it go for the fourth stone is Indifference which goes well with Ignorance—they are a common excuse, one taking the blame for the other. Ignorance only requires your attention but Indifference requires nothing at all. The fourth stone is always reliable. The fourth stone is a way out. The fourth stone is the most popular stone of all. With this stone you can fill the pit with excuses for every kind of evil.

And that is almost all you need. But wait, there is the fifth stone, a dull yellow color and smaller than the rest. But still it guards the pit and you must shove it in to see what it contains. The fifth stone is Jealousy and it is what will keep you searching in every corner of the world where there are always those with more than you. It will nullify trust and sour the milk you drink. It will vandalize love and keep the taste of bitterness in your mouth. With this stone you can fill the pit with rage, blaming everyone in your life.

The pit is the opposite side of the Idea and once in it, you cannot get out. The pit is deep and has no steps, only tunnels opened by the stones and they lead to variations on the stones. But they will not lead you out.

Stand back and look at the One Idea Having Opposite Sides, the Old Man shouted to the Moon-Faced Dog. Do you choose the lake or the pit?

Neither, the Moon-Faced Dog shouted back. I choose the path which is emerging but it is no choice at all. It is inevitable.

The Old Man saw that it was true. He saw that there

was nothing else for the Moon-Faced Dog to do. The Old Man said, both sides of the Idea are in me all the time. Both sides are clamoring to be heard. Both sides appear to be the right side, depending on where I stand. There are days when I choose the lake, there are days when I choose the pit, being blinded by the stones. There are days when I do not choose either one.

The Moon-Faced Dog shook his head. I cannot choose for I am the absence of One Idea.

I am the world before it came.

I am nature dispossessed of conscience.

I am nature dispossessed of will.

I am nature dispossessing man.

I am instinct and survival and patterns too old to be changed.

I am born without thought or reason.

I am never alone for all things are present in me.

The Old Man looked at the Moon-Faced Dog and saw him for the first time. He saw winter summoning summer and he saw night summoning day. He saw the ocean summoning the river and he saw the earth summoning all. The Old Man began to tremble for he saw at last the true nature of the Moon-Faced Dog.

You are the Spirit of the Corn, the Old Man said in surprise. It is you who have been in me all along. Because of you I am able to make the corn grow. Because of you the fire does not go out. Because of you there is a story to tell.

Nonsense, said the Moon-Faced Dog. I have obliged you with my presence, that is all. I listened to you but nothing at all has changed, for words cannot contribute change to me.

The Old Man understood then the futility of words. He

understood that his story had no effect on the Moon-Faced Dog but that the Moon-Faced Dog would have an effect on his story from now on.

What shall I do? the Old Man asked the Moon-Faced Dog who was gathering up the shadow he had left.

What you have always done, said the Moon-Faced Dog. There is a story to be told. You can tell it or not tell it. You can forget everything and go home.

The Moon-Faced Dog was growing smaller and smaller. His tail stopped wagging and pointed in the direction of the water flowing down. His face had begun to eclipse. There was darkness moving across it, eating up the expression that he wore.

The Old Man watched what was happening to the Moon-Faced Dog and he said:

I know who I am and it is the right person.

I know where I am and it is the right place.

I know what I know and it is the right sort of knowledge.

All this is so because I believe it to be so. There is but one path for me to follow and one end already begun.

You have finally told the right story, said the Moon-Faced Dog. Now you may or may not be heard. You may or may not make a difference in the world.

I no longer care, the Old Man said. The important thing is, I have made a difference in myself. I have raised my deepest shadows to the sun.

The Moon-Faced Dog had recognized his path and he followed it in the only way he could go, which was downward, in the same direction as the stream, for he was of the same energy as the stream and had the same destination inside him. The Moon-Faced Dog went with the stream with neither question nor resistance. It was time for him to go and he departed in the only way he could.

But the Old Man began to walk upward, in the direction of the top; his nature was of growth and he could not go down. He walked against the flow of water and the hold of gravity, seeking to contradict the laws which were always present. The Old Man's roots were deeply planted and they held him fast as he made his way higher and higher, seeking to find the sun which was coming up.

Full Circle

ONE FOOTSTEP
GOING ON

The Old Man went without food and water, for his sustenance was within him. He remained in his Being as a man for he was in search of a vision; a vision was what the Old Man needed before he could take another Being as his own. The Old Man sat on top of the Mountain and prayed to the sun and the moon and the stars and to the earth which accepted him. The Old Man's song was a song of thanksgiving; it was a song of praise and a song of preparation. The music lifted the Old Man's spirit which contained the Spirit of the Corn and so he began to grow for he perceived himself as an ear of corn with his energy flowing out of the rock and up the stalk. The tassel that was connected to each kernel of corn was the way in which his energy and his pollen and his knowledge were passed throughout the world.

The Old Man built a Fire and surrounded it with stones and enclosed it with aspen trees so that Smoke was contained in the womb he had made. The Old Man in his nakedness climbed into the womb and was confronted by Fire and Smoke and the heat of the stones. His sweat poured out into the womb and the poisons that were in him were received by Smoke. The Old Man's body was cleansed by Fire and Smoke; it was cleansed by the earth that he painted onto himself.

The Old Man was surrounded by Fire and within it his anger burned out; within it his Ancestors rose and fell from one lifetime into the next and he could see their natures changing and dissolving until at last he saw only Smoke coming from the lifetimes they had left.

Then in the Smoke, the Old Man saw the end of the earth by Fire. He saw everything dead and burning. He saw the Smoke rise and take with it the effort of mankind. He saw nature absolved of its gift. The Old Man saw the sun turn blue; he saw the moon turn red and fall.

In the ruined earth there was no wholeness left and amid the crumbled mountains and the rivers of ash the Old Man saw no movement. He saw mankind lying face down upon the earth. He saw the breath of the earth consumed by Fire and Smoke victorious over all.

But as the Old Man watched, a certain dark form began to move up from the ruined earth. The form first rested upon its hands and knees; then it looked around and saw the earth in desolation. The form began to sink back down for it saw there was no hope. The Old Man saw that it was a human form and he shouted to it.

Get up, the Old Man cried. But he could see there was no reason for getting up. He could see that the earth had perished.

The human form raised its head slowly to the sky which was yellow and filled with Smoke and it smelled the smell of death on the wind which was lifeless. The human form looked down at the earth which was wet with blood and the rivers which had turned to dust. The human form saw bones in the dust and feathers coming down from the sky. The human form lay back down in the scorched and ruined earth and covered itself with a blanket of blood, assuming the position of birth, choosing it for the position of death. A prolonged cry of anguish came from the human form and the Old Man recognized it as the whole of mankind crying. He recognized it as sorrow and shame.

The human form lay still and lifeless and Smoke covered it but the Old Man saw that part of the earth still burned. There was still Fire because there was still air and out of the Fire, rising and curling like Smoke, the Old Man saw the Thread and was amazed for there was no expectation to it.

The Thread came over to where the human form lay and rested above it until at last it began to rise and rock slowly back and forth on its hands and knees. Then the human form began to stand on its feet, reaching out toward the space in front of it that was dark with Smoke. It was a space that contained the Thread but the human form did not see the Thread at all. The Old Man realized that the human form was blind.

You have feet, the Old Man cried. They were meant to go forward. If they were meant to go backward, they would be turned the other way.

The human form turned its hollow eyes toward the devastation, trying to see through its blindness. The human form raised its arms to the sky and cried to it, yearning for touch and support. The Old Man saw that the Thread answered the human cry and came and touched the hands of blindness. But what the human form held was not the Thread at all but a single perfect flower.

The human held the flower in its hands and took one

step forward and stopped, crying, where is the path? I am blind and cannot find my way.

In the distance there was the sound of water running over rock. There was the sound of wind starting up again. There was the song of a lonely bird in a tree. There was the sound of another footstep.

The human form began to walk toward it.

I am one footstep going on, the human form said. I am going on to find another footstep. And when there are two footsteps, we will both go on.

Then the Old Man heard all the voices of mankind saying the same thing:

I am one footstep going on.

The Old Man heard all of the footsteps of mankind going on and it sounded like an army, thundering across the land. The Old Man heard them singing:

We are one footstep going on.

The Old Man heard the silence broken.

When the Old Man had completed his vision and come out of the womb and dressed himself in his red blanket and put on his feathers and his moccasins, he stood alone against the sky which was pure and new with morning. He gave thanks and made an attitude toward the day and addressed the Mountain which had been in him all that time.

I have come to the end of seeing and believing, the Old Man said. I have come to the end of my Circle.

You will never come to the end of your Circle, the Mountain said. You will never come to the end of seeing or believing because you will never come to the end of being. Your blood is made of mud and eggshells and bone. Listen to what your blood tells you. Your feet which have taken you everywhere are the fins of a fish. Listen to what your feet tell you. Your wings which carry you out of your world are the wings of a bird that died before I was born. Listen to what your wings tell you. Your heart is the heart of a fish who swam until the ocean dried up. Listen to what your heart tells you.

Looking out across the land, the Old Man saw that there were lizards and fish and frogs marooned on dry land, caught in the Seam between the earth and the sky. The creatures longed for the mud. It was where they had come from and their new surroundings were unfamiliar to them. The Old Man saw that they looked to the sky for water. It is a good sign, he thought. Before, their eyes were always on the ground.

The Mountain looked in another direction. What the Mountain saw was a swamp where the top of the lizards was in the shape of a man. The fish walked about on legs. The frogs had arms with which to pull food from the trees.

The Mountain said, there. They do not pretend that the desert is a swamp. They have accepted the place where they have found themselves. They are working with it.

As the Mountain and the Old Man watched, the creatures reached up and pulled the Thread from the sky.

The Old Man and the Mountain looked out and they saw in the distance another mountain where all their Ancestors were. They saw that their Ancestors were building a road into the mountain, into the heart which which was the home of Fire.

It is hopeless, the Old Man said. There are too many layers to go.

The Mountain said, they are working and that is the important thing.

What do they find at the end? the Old Man asked.

The beginning, the Mountain replied.

The Old Man flew off then on the East Wind, out and over the land, past the desert and the swamp and the mountain where his Ancestors were. He flew in a great Circle, flying in and out of light and dark, flying in and out of Fire. He flew into both worlds in and out of time and he flew into time and saw it in all directions.

At last the Old Man dropped to the Seam which lay between the World of the Earth and the World of the Sky. The Seam was where mankind lived between the two forever trying to perceive the nature of each.

The sky, which was stronger because it had the sun and the moon living in it, was always pulling at the earth. The sky was always coaxing the earth to come into its home which had no limitation. The earth, which was wiser because it consisted of things which knew how to grow, was always pulling at the sky. The earth was always coaxing the sky to come into its home which was always changing. The Seam was where the World of the Earth and the World of the Sky met one another. It was where they deliberated and where they schemed to win one over the other. It was where they created a truce from time to time.

When the sky was angry with the earth, it sent rain and snow to cover it. When the earth was angry with the sky, it sent smoke and dust to annoy it. The sky had a way of sending the earth too much just as the earth had a way of yielding too little to the sky. The sky had clouds and darkness to conceal it from the earth. The earth had mist and smoke to keep it from the total vision of the sky.

The Seam was where all of this was happening all of the

time and would go on happening until either the sky or the earth won the struggle between them. One day either the sky or the earth would disappear entirely.

The Old Man was happy when he found himself at the Seam. He was ready to dwell there as long as he could. The Seam was the Old Man's habitat.

Because he had been gone so long, the Old Man had missed the Seam. It was a place of war and confusion but he loved it all the same. He looked around and saw the green fields that he had not seen for a long time; he saw People of the Sun House Moon who were familiar to him and some who were not; he saw that although he had been away for a long time, nothing had changed in his absence. The river was where he remembered it and the Mountain was as beautiful as ever; the sky was the same hard blue and his village was made of earth and glistened in the sun. The Old Man took a deep breath and found that it was good to be where he was with everything before him. The Old Man was happy to be home.

The Old Man lived quietly among the People of the Sun House Moon for a long time, teaching them how to plant, for the Spirit of the Corn was in him and he was able to make things grow. He gave them the gift of Fire and he stood guard over it so that it never went out nor was stolen nor spread farther than the village itself. The Old Man and the Fire were always side by side. Even in the dark, everyone could tell where the Old Man was.

This time the Old Man did not want to do any more than guard the Fire and make the corn grow; his story was inside him but he had no desire to get it out.

If someone asks to hear my story, I will give it to them,

the Old Man said. Otherwise I shall keep it to myself. There is too much pain in telling.

Every morning just before it was light, the Old Man came out of his house made of earth and stood on his roof, turning his eyes toward the path of the rising sun. He saw that the Morning Star was in her place and that all was as it should be in order for the sun to come up. Every morning the Old Man gave thanks and prepared a greeting for the sun. It was an ancient greeting and he spoke it reverently. He spoke the greeting until the sun was safely up in the sky.

A layer of thin blue smoke always hung over the village and the golden light of dawn streamed through it. The smoke and the light gave a rich haziness to the land which was dry and waiting for rain. The Old Man was also waiting for rain and the dance that he did every morning was an ancient dance; the dance was necessary in order for rain to come to the dry land and the Old Man. The dance was part of the Old Man's expression. The dance opened to the Old Man the possibility of rain.

The New People came and went in the Old Man's village the way they always did, taking pictures of him the way they always had before. But the Old Man never spoke to them any more. He sat where he was, in front of his Fire, waiting for the people to speak to him. But the New People were always silent.

One day in the fall of the year, when the harvest was nearly complete, and the People of the Sun House Moon were getting ready for the fiesta again, some New People came to visit the Old Man in his house made of earth. They climbed up his ladder and knocked on his door.

The Old Man asked them to come in and sit down. He asked them to come to his fire.

Tell us, they said politely, what life is like here. Looking around, they saw that it was very dusty and drab. They saw that they were better off living where they were. They began to remember the places they had left and were anxious to get back to them.

Every day there is something good to see, the Old Man said, seating himself by the Fire. Sometimes the fields are so green that they cover the mind with wetness. Sometimes the corn is big enough to crawl inside to see the way it is growing. Sometimes the water runs backward, taking us up to the place of its birth. Sometimes the rainbow breaks in two and a butterfly comes out of the middle.

The Fire crackled and leapt up. The Fire had some chance of surviving as long as the Old Man talked.

The people were restless in the house which was made of mud. They were surrounded by the World of the Earth on six sides. The essence of the earth poured in on them from all directions at once without touching them. They saw only the dust falling from a crack in the ceiling. The people longed to go back where they came from. They listened to the Old Man but they did not hear him at first. They did not feel the warmth of his Fire.

The Old Man looked at the New People and saw that they were straining their necks to see something. His blood began to whisper to him and he felt his feet stir in the mud of the house. Something was happening to the people who were looking up.

The Old Man remembered the lizards and the fish and the frogs who had come out of the slime onto dry land. He remembered how they longed to go back to the slime. But the time had come for them to be separated from it. They could not go back to the slime no matter how hard they tried. The Old Man remembered the first time he had seen them look to the sky for water. Before, their eyes were always on the ground.

The people were looking up at the crack which was like a crack in the earth seen from the bottom side. They were fascinated with the idea of the house which was made of mud. They began to look at it carefully. Although they had never been to the Old Man's house before, the people sensed something about it.

One man, who was accustomed to traveling around, spoke first. He said, you have built a strong house.

The next man, who was used to measuring things, said, everything fits very well together. The roof is neither too high nor too low.

The third man, who was used to reading books, said, houses rise and fall. This house rose from the earth and will fall into the earth. There is no difference between them.

The Old Man smiled. I am in need of a Match, he said. A Match is the only way to find out.

The three men gave him Matches and he saw that the flames were equal.

The people looked at one another and wondered what had happened. During the lifetime of each flame they had seen something they had not seen before.

The man who was accustomed to traveling around saw the water running backward, up the Mountain to the place of its birth. He went a little way with it which was as far as he could go without becoming worn out from so much effort.

The man who was used to measuring things saw that the corn was wide enough for him to crawl through. When he got to the center of it he was able to stand up and look around. He did not take a step because he could not see how much room there was.

The man who was used to reading books saw the butterfly coming out of the rainbow. He saw that it was every color that the rainbow was and that its wings were as wide as the sky. He rode the butterfly himself, but not too high, for the earth was a long way below.

The first man said, how far can you go with the water running backward?

The Old Man said, you can go as far as you like.

The first man said, suppose it is too difficult?

The Old Man said, once you have started, there is no choice. You must go all the way to the end.

The second man said, how much room is there in the corn?

The Old Man said, there is as much room as you need. The inside of the corn is limitless.

The second man said, suppose I become lost inside?

The Old Man said, there is always that chance. Still, once you are inside the corn, it will not matter.

The third man said, how high can the butterfly travel without falling to the earth?

The Old Man said, to the other half of the rainow. To the half which lies on the other side of the sky.

The third man said, no one has ever come back from there. Suppose I lose sight of the earth?

The Old Man said, do not worry. You are attached to the earth. The earth will travel with you.

They looked at one another, not knowing what to believe. They had begun to feel comfortable in the Old Man's house. They had begun to understand the elusiveness of his face. Yet they were not certain of where they found themselves; they were disconnected from everything they knew.

The first man said, it is growing late.

The second man said, it is growing dark.

The third man said, it is growing cold.

But the Old Man said, it is growing and that is the important thing.

The Fire was burning brightly and the people turned their eyes toward it, held fast by its mysterious light. The people reached out their hands to the Fire and felt the warmth in their fingertips spread to the bottoms of their feet.

The crackling of the Fire made the people look over their shoulders at something which called to them without assurance or recognition. The crackling of the Fire seemed to contain a rhythm. The people listened to it carefully and heard a cry from a bird they thought extinct.

Then they stood up and went outside and turned their faces to the sky in order to watch for the bird they thought extinct. They reached up and pulled the Thread from the sky.

The Old Man hurried from his house which was made of mud and passed through his village in the sun, calling to the People of the Sun House Moon. The Old Man went to his fields which had been harvested except for a single stalk of corn and he prayed to the cornstalk and to the Corn Spirit, perceiving the Moon-Faced Dog sitting at the edge of the field, watching him, wagging his tail in a continuous circle.

It is the way it has been done ever since the first stalk of corn, the Old Man said and drew his knife.

But the Moon-Faced Dog said nothing for he knew what was to come. When the Old Man raised his knife to cut the last stalk of the corn, the Moon-Faced Dog became part of the tassel and the Old Man saw him die at the moment the cornstalk died.

It is finished, the Old Man said. And he laid the tassel carefully in the ground.

The People turned to thank the Old Man, for they had accepted his story and were strengthened by it. They looked at where the Old Man had been standing beside the Fire but all they saw was a little pile of ash, blowing away in the wind.

Where has the Old Man gone? the people asked for they were concerned about him. They called for him but since he had no name, they could only call certain words which had no meaning. When they decided he was not in his house, the people went outside and stood on the roof, trying to find the Old Man among the People of the Sun House Moon who were moving about in the plaza.

Where has the Old Man gone? the people asked again, thinking that something had happened to him. We wish to hear the rest of his story. We wish him to tell us some more.

As they began to climb down the Old Man's ladder, the people stopped and looked at the sun which was beginning to grow dark with rain clouds. The people heard Thunder rolling out from a cloud which was shaped like a buffalo; they heard Thunder coming from the top of the Mountain; they heard Thunder coming from the wings of a beautiful Silver Bird flying out away from the storm. It was the bird they thought extinct.

Thunder, the people said. Thunder. And they began to speak about Thunder in a language that was just coming into being: they listened to Thunder for it seemed to contain a voice they could understand.

The people held on to the Thread and went out into the world, listening to the Thunder which grew louder and louder in their ears, blocking out the thoughts they had come there with.

From that day on, whenever the people of the world heard Thunder, they heard one other sound besides.

They heard one footstep going on.

About the Author

Nancy Wood grew up in New Jersey but moved to Colorado a number of years ago. Long fascinated by the heritage and culture of native Americans, Ms. Wood has written two books about the Taos Pueblo Indians, *Hollering Sun* and *Many Winters*, as well as a libretto, *War Cry on a Prayer Feather*. Her novels include *The King of Liberty Bend* and *The Last Five Dollar Baby*. With Roy Emerson Stryker, she produced *In This Proud Land: A Photographic Look at America, 1935–1943*. In 1976 the Colorado Centennial Bicentennial Commission awarded her a grant to photograph the rural people of the state. Ms. Wood now lives in Colorado Springs, Colorado, and is at work on a book about the Ute Indians.